Allie stood and led her upstairs to their bedroom. In the moonlit room they slowly undressed each other, Brett unable to touch Allie enough. Allie laid Brett down on the bed, her naked flesh warm on Brett's.

Brett enjoyed Allie's curves, the supple softness of her breasts, the scent of her arousal. She rolled Allie onto her back and worked her way down her body, over the soft skin of her throat, to hardened nipples, which she teased back and forth between her teeth, over her slender belly, taking her time to play her tongue over Allie's navel ring.

She then moved down to Allie's feet, first one and then the other, sucking at her toes before kissing and licking her way up lightly muscled calves and thighs. She spread Allie's legs, sitting up between them and running her hands down over her stomach into the thick patch of blond hair before burying herself in Allie's wetness.

She needed to be inside Allie, and Brett always took what she needed.

LOOKING FOR NAIAD?

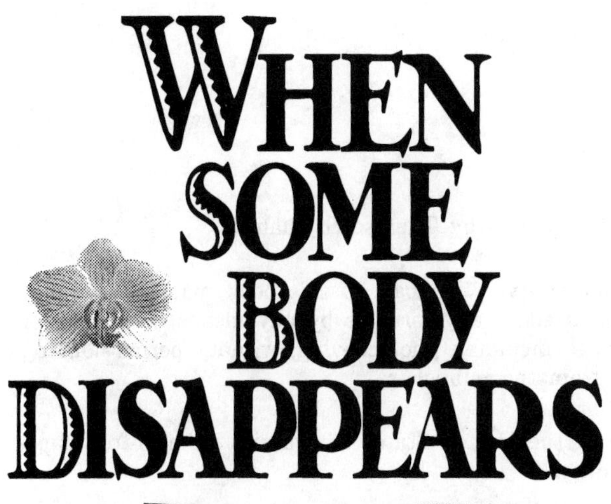

THERESE SZYMANSKI

THE NAIAD PRESS, INC.
1999

Printed in the United States of America on acid-free paper
First Edition

Editor: Christine Cassidy
Cover designer: Bonnie Liss (Phoenix Graphics)
Typesetter: Sandi Stancil

Library of Congress Cataloging-in-Publication Data

Szymanski, Therese, 1968 –
When some body disappears : the third Brett Higgins mystery / by Therese Szymanski.
p. cm.
ISBN 1-56280-227-5 (alk. paper)
I. Title.
PS3569.Z94W476 1998
813′.54—dc21 98-31632
CIP

Dedication

This one is for all the incredible Naiad women, from Barbara and Donna, who decided to take a chance on "a Polish baby dyke from the Motor City," to Christi Cassidy (a.k.a. the "Editor Goddess"), who didn't throw in the towel during the rewrite of this book. Also in this group are Sandi, the typesetter; Bonnie, with her jacket designs; Kathleen, for the jacket copy; and all the rest of the staff, Alex, Tori, Charity, Ricki, and Kelly (of course!).

I'd also like to thank Naiad writer Barbara Johnson, as well as Kathy and Andrea, Hawk and TJ and Jan and Parri, all of whom helped pull me down from extreme levels of mania in the middle of the night when everything was going wrong, showing me what real friends are.

Thank you all!

About the Author

Therese Szymanski has kept a roof over her head doing a little bit of almost everything — from fast food, cooking, waiting tables, security, investigation, media buying and planning, copywriting, managing an adult theater with a bookstore and distributorship, to being an Army reservist. She now works in computer tech support.

She has always lived in Michigan and enjoys cruising the local bars and hanging out in extremely unsavory neighborhoods, although she still refuses to share most of her past until the second date.

Prologue

Brett parked her car, smoothed back her short, black hair, looked at herself through Ray-Ban-protected eyes in the rearview mirror, pulled on her soft, black leather gloves, picked up the attaché case and immediately went into the theater where the clerk let her into the box office. From there she headed to the suite of offices upstairs. Before she even took off her long trenchcoat or black silk scarf, she went into Rick's office and deftly opened the hidden safe. She set the black leather briefcase on the floor, undid the lock and emptied the thousands of dollars into the safe. Only when the money was secured did she go into her own office, toss the nearly empty briefcase on her desk, hang up her coat and scarf and pour herself a Glenfiddich single-malt scotch on the rocks.

As she always did when she entered her office, she looked at the pictures on her bookcase. She smiled as she gazed at Storm's features and her sweet smile. Gone but not forgotten . . .Would she ever forget the vivacious Storm? Even though Storm had been dead for a couple of years now, Brett still thought of her every day, remembered how it was to hold her and love her.

And then there was the picture of the beautiful blue-eyed blond, Allison Sullivan. If Brett had lost Storm to death, she had lost Allie to her own stupidity; if she thought about Storm daily, then she thought about Allie hourly. She lovingly examined every detail of Allie's face, although she already had the classic features and aristocratic nose firmly imprinted on every cell of her brain.

A longing as familiar as breathing consumed her soul with an often denied need for love and passion. No other woman had ever made her feel this way. Although their relationship hadn't even lasted a year, its demise had left Brett feeling as if a Mack truck had totaled her very core.

She took a long pull on her drink, enjoying the way the scotch burned a trail down her throat and into her stomach, killing all feeling in its path, and turned back to her desk. She popped the briefcase open and took out the papers. As she sat, she unconsciously straightened the crease of her pants and noticed a splattering of red on the silky fabric.

"Goddamnit! The fuckhead bled on me!" she cursed, going to retrieve some soda water from the bar. Not only did the asshole try to withhold money, but he had the nerve to bleed on her while she persuaded him that honesty was the best policy. Perhaps he was due a little visit from Frankie, who highly disapproved of such poor behavior. Frankie could easily show him the error of his ways, a lesson he wouldn't soon forget if it forced him to spend a week in the I.C.U.

She had just started going through the paperwork when Kirsten entered. Brett glanced up only long enough to see who it was before she returned to her work, heedless of the naked woman standing in her doorway.

Kirsten strode over and sat on Brett's lap with her legs spread wide, one leg on either side of Brett. Brett leaned back and looked at Kirsten's long auburn hair, automatically putting her hands on Kirsten's naked thighs, up above the thigh-high fishnet stockings.

With a soft, sultry smile, Kirsten suggestively ran her tongue over her lips. Her nipples were already hard and swollen, the aureoles puckered. She tried to take Brett's hands up to her breasts, but Brett stopped at her waist.

Brett could smell Kirsten's arousal. The woman had just gotten off stage, just finished giving lap dances and had come to Brett for satisfaction and to forget the feel of the men's hands upon her.

But Brett was in a dour mood and didn't like it that Kirsten assumed she could just stroll in as if they loved each other or were a couple. Get real. Kirsten was an easy fuck, a quick scratch to the itch Brett occasionally felt.

"Shit, Kirsten, leave me the fuck alone," Brett complained, pushing her away with a snarl.

"I love it when you talk dirty to me."

"Brett," Rick DeSilva suddenly said from the open doorway, "when you get a moment, come into my office. There's somebody I'd like you to meet." Brett looked around Kirsten and saw her boss standing next to a tall, deeply tanned, dark-haired man. She guessed he'd be considered a real hunk if you liked that sort of thing. He was giving her a sly look, and she knew he wouldn't think twice about giving Kirsten a quick run across the mattress.

"Kirsten, I got work to do." Brett unceremoniously dumped Kirsten on the floor, then followed Rick and the stranger into Rick's office. Frankie, Rick's other lieutenant, followed too.

"Brett, I'd like you to meet an old friend of mine — Antonio Marzetti," Rick said.

"Anybody who treats a woman like that can call me Tony." The man grinned and stuck out a large, meaty hand. "Nice to meet you. Rick's told me all about you."

Brett looked into his eyes and realized she didn't like the fellow. He was too calm, too cool, too collected — no one was really that composed. He was a well-polished façade, not human at all. She ignored his hand and instead gave him her best go-fuck-yourself look. "I don't know about you, but I never believe a word that son-of-a-bitch says." She said it without humor, although she loved Rick like the father she wished she'd had.

Rick laughed, and the man took a step back and crossed his arms over his chest. "I've got some bad news, though," he said. "Now that you know who I am, I'll have to kill you, even though I like you."

Even as Brett pulled herself up to her full five feet ten inches, she could almost hear Frankie bristling behind her: he didn't like this fellow any more than she did. She started to reach for the .357 in her shoulder holster. Her eyes darted from Tony to Rick, and on Rick's face she saw a smirk wending its way over the features she knew so well.

Rick said, "Tony, it's a miracle you're still standing. Brett usually don't take too kindly to remarks like that."

"Hey, honey, I was just joking that nobody knows who I am."

"Tone," Rick interjected before Brett had a chance to, "you're about to eat your balls for dinner."

"That's if he's got any," Brett replied. "Which I sincerely doubt."

Rick threw an arm about Tony's shoulder in camaraderie. "Brett, I know he can be a jerk," he said before Tony could throw anything back at Brett, "but I thought you'd like to meet a man who is well on his way to becoming a legend in the field."

Tony leisurely lit a cigar and made himself right at home. He chuckled. "Well, I might be a legend if anybody knew who I was."

"The people that matter know enough," Rick said.

"What do you mean?" Brett asked finally.

"I'm what you might call a freelance artist — I work on individual contracts. And I work under different names and identities, so that the authorities can never find out too much about me."

"So you're a hit man."

He laughed. It was an annoying sound. "I prefer to think of myself as an harbinger of Hades. And it has to be more than just a hit for me to accept it as a suitable proposition."

"You mean it's got to pay enough, or be a big enough feather in your cap for you to lower yourself to doing actual work."

Tony laughed at her. "Maybe someday you'll be in a position to choose your own work."

Brett stood just far enough away so she didn't have to look up at him. "I already do."

Rick strolled over to the bar to pour them all a drink. "He's in town on business — you may have heard about his most recent job, Brett." He wasn't a man who got nervous, ever.

Brett looked at Tony curiously. It was obvious that Rick held Tony in esteem, although she couldn't figure out why, but in Brett's estimation that alone was enough to give him some stature.

"Let's just say it involved a few bombs," Tony said cryptically, sending recent headlines flying through Brett's head. She knew too well about his latest "job" at one of the automakers. She was surprised he was cocky enough to stay in town after that one. He was looking to get busted.

Over the next several hours Brett learned more than she cared to about Rick and Tony's outrageous boyhood together — complete with full details on all the pranks they played — and it cemented her dislike of this walking, talking caricature. She really didn't care who he was connected to, who he had ever worked for or who he drank with. She didn't care about his big plans for the future either.

"After all, a man can't go on doin' this forever.

Takes a young man to do all this climbing, crawling and running, and you and me ain't gettin' any younger, Rick."

A year later, Rick had to remind her of his old friend when he did another job in Detroit — Rick recognized his work from the style of the bombing, but all Brett could think of was the long scar that snaked its way down across his cheek like an *S*.

Chapter One

Four Years Later

With jagged breath and bent knees, Brett slammed her skis to the right and launched herself up into the air, the cold cutting against her face and through her hair as she flew through the air, adrenaline rushing through her system. Her skis hit the snow and she brought herself up, racing forward as she cut her skis to the side, coming to a quick hockey-stop.

Her heart still beating fast, she turned to look up

the slope at Allie, who grinned at her from the top. Allie's long, lean figure gracefully raced down toward her, long blond hair billowing out behind her as she skillfully edged her skis from side to side, speeding toward the jump at the bottom of the slope. Like an eagle, she looked free when she was in the air. She was beautiful. Every morning when she woke up next to her, Brett couldn't help but think just how lucky she was, or how ironic it was that a cop who had wanted to kill her ended up returning Allie to her instead.

But Brett didn't have a chance to tell Allie this, or even to fully enjoy the moment, because as soon as Allie's skis hit the ground she was racing off to the left, a huge smile plastered across her face as she flew past Brett.

"Again!"

Brett dropped the tips of her skis downhill and skated down the slope, trying to build the momentum to carry her over the slight uphill rise, sweat breaking out on her brow as she fought to catch up. Allie was a better skier, but Brett had been hitting the runs all morning while Allie went to her Aunt Gertrude's 90th birthday celebration. The Mineshaft was the only really challenging run that Alpine Valley, located in White Lake, Michigan, had to offer.

She cut to the left and hit the hill going full speed. She pushed off the top and her skis sliced into the air as she passed just over Allie's head, leaning forward to maintain her balance for landing. When she hit the ground several feet in front of Allie, she swerved just in time to miss another skier coming in from a different run. She gracefully swished in and out, edging just enough to keep control while maintaining her lead on Allie, glancing back once to see Allie's blond hair. She smiled at the sight.

She loved the thrill of zipping over the ground on her waxed skis, loved the excitement of shooting into the air during jumps, the challenge of new slopes and new adventures, and the competition with herself and others. Nothing could compare to straining her body to its limits as adrenaline pumped through her system and she whipped along, the cold air nipping at her nose and ears, the snow blowing into her face, and the feeling of success after each new obstacle was overcome.

"I'm glad I decided to come down with you," Brett said once they were on the chairlift. She playfully tapped Allie's ski tips with her own as she put her arm around Allie's shoulders.

"So am I." Allie smiled. "No problems, I take it?"

"Nah, I told you it wouldn't be a problem. Anyway, who the hell would recognize me dressed like this?" Brett was on the lam, having switched her name to Samantha Peterson and moved with Allie to Alma, Michigan, a town two hours north of her native Detroit. Even in what was technically a suburb of Detroit, she was out in the boonies as far as she was concerned.

Allie nodded, but Brett couldn't see her eyes because of the tinted goggles she had on. It was a gorgeous Saturday afternoon that Brett wanted to enjoy. Even though all the snow was the crappy man-made sort you get at the end of the season, it was a miracle they were skiing in April, and Brett was happy, especially because it was one of her last days of freedom before starting her new job on Monday.

When they first went on the lam about a year and a half ago, they moved to California but discovered, much to their surprise, that they missed Michigan with its ever-changing seasons and beautiful fall colors. That was when they risked moving back to Michigan, but far enough away from Detroit, where Brett had once been a member of a criminal organization. When she got out of the business, she changed her name and sold her holdings to her old partner, Frankie Lorenzini. Between that sale and all the money she made during her career, she had enough money to live fairly comfortably for almost the rest of her life.

Allie laughed. "I can't quite imagine your old pals hanging around ski slopes anyway."

They both looked up just in time to disembark from the lift. Brett paused to pull her pole straps onto her wrists, but Allie flew by her to the left, and Brett raced off after her.

"Catch me if you can!" Allie yelled over her shoulder at the top of the Mineshaft before pushing her weight forward and firmly planting her poles into the snow. With a wild *whoop* she pushed herself off the ledge and down the nearly vertical slope. Brett stood watching Allie, who skillfully schusced down the slope, her skis perfectly parallel as she maneuvered over the moguls, her rear end wiggling enticingly as she kept her shoulders to the fall line, moving only her lower half to accommodate the changing terrain of the steep run.

Another skier came from Brett's left and jumped off the edge and onto the slope, where he promptly wiped out and tumbled down to the bottom of the slope in a jumble of poles, skis, goggles and gloves. He looked like a broken toy some disgruntled kid had tossed aside.

Brett planted her poles into the snow and pushed off, hitting the air only to pound into another mogul as she sped forward, the powder hitting her goggles as she carved into the turns.

Allie finished the run and stood watching Brett, who laid into her edges when she pulled up in a perfect hockey stop, spraying Allie's pants and skis with a light cover of wet snow. Allie grimaced.

"Meet you at the bottom," Brett dared, pushing off to a skating start down the mountain. She shifted her weight quickly, gaining momentum as she tried to outrun Allie. She bent low, tucking her poles under her arms as she went into a racer's crouch.

Just before the lodge, Allie skied up alongside her. "Show-off," she said.

"You ready for lunch?" Brett asked with a raised eyebrow.

They locked up their skis and poles, loosened their boots and headed inside for an over-priced lodge meal. As they were sitting at a table with their food, Brett caught something out of the corner of her eye.

"Oh, shit," she mumbled, frozen in place.

"What's the matter, hon?" Allie asked, concern weaving its way over her fine features as she followed Brett's gaze across the crowded room.

A throng of beautiful bunnies were gathered around a tall, deeply tanned, dark-haired man dressed in matching royal blue ski jacket and bibs. He looked confident, sure of himself, like he knew what he was doing on the slopes and in the bedroom. A cockeyed pig, Brett thought. He glanced up, noticed Allie and shot her a knowing smile, the scar on his cheek stretching with the change in his expression.

"Don't let him see you!" Brett warned, quickly adjusting her seat so her back was to him.

"Who is he?" Allie whispered curiously, breaking her gaze at him to look at Brett.

"Two such beauties, all alone . . ." the man said, pulling up a chair and straddling it. "Perhaps I can help alleviate your aloneness on this fine spring day?" He was looking directly at Allie while Brett busily spread mayo, butter, ketchup, horseradish, Ranch dressing, hot sauce and mustard on her turkey salad sandwich. "My name is Guy, Guy Franklin," he added, casually resting his hand on Allie's.

"And I'm —" Allie removed her hand from under his as she fumbled for a name. "I'm Liza Swanson, and this is my friend . . . my friend Jen McDonald," she concluded, using names from their recent past. She apparently realized that Brett didn't want him to have any idea who they were and that even the name Samantha Peterson could be tracked.

"Jen McDonald . . ." Guy mused, looking over at Brett, who quickly dove under the table after a napkin she had just fumbled. "Don't I know you from somewhere?" he continued, watching her closely.

"I don't think so . . ." Brett said with a heavy Southern drawl. "You're not from down South, are you?"

"No, but I know I like the Southern belles just fine."

Before Brett could even try to get Allie out of there, or communicate anything at all to her, another man walked up behind Guy and planted a hand on his shoulder. Uglier than a constipated pit bull, he wore goggles and a hat, a tan parka and bluejeans. He clutched his leather gloves in one hand and looked ill at ease in the bulky ski boots, as if he didn't belong there and didn't particularly want to be there. "Guy Franklin?" he said. "Chester Bombast. Long time no see."

Guy looked up at the mysterious intruder. "Nice boots. Are they European?" he asked, never looking at Chester's feet.

"Like my skis, they're Italian."

"But it's the Swiss who know how to telemark."

Brett dumped her soda onto the table and said in mock horror, "Ooops! I am such a klutz!"

Chester glanced at her. "Do I know you?"

Brett grabbed Allie by the arm. "Help me get the stain out." She jumped up and dragged Allie behind her.

"Ditz," Guy mumbled as they rushed off.

Brett pulled Allie off toward the bathrooms but quickly dodged to the side once they were in the hallway. She stood peering out at the two men.

"What's going on?" Allie exclaimed as Brett watched the men from her hiding spot. Chester handed Guy a large envelope that had been secreted in his parka. Guy opened it up and pulled out a smaller envelope that to Brett's trained eye could very well be filled with cash. A pretty nice sum of cash. Guy slipped this envelope into his pocket and pulled a printed sheet from the larger envelope, reading it with his brow furrowed in concentration. Chester appeared to be explaining something to him as Guy slowly nodded and smiled.

"Let's get the fuck outta here!" Brett growled, pulling Allie out the side door.

"Don't you think you're being a little paranoid?" Allie asked Brett later that night. All their ski gear was packed in the Explorer Frankie had bought for them on their return to Michigan. Now, on their way home they had stopped at Clara's on Michigan Avenue in Lansing for a nice dinner.

"Paranoia, my dear, would be if I thought they were out to get me. I do not think that. I was merely afraid they would recognize me," Brett patiently explained. She wondered whether Allie would ever fully understand who she had been, what she had done, or what she knew from her past life. Although Allie knew most of the details of it and had helped her develop a new identity, sometimes it didn't seem like she grasped all the implications of it. Brett had been a criminal, a leading name in Detroit's organized crime circles.

"So what if they did?" Allie asked, clearly frustrated with Brett's covers, innuendoes and secrecy.

"Honey," Brett said, taking Allie's hand lightly. "We both know it's best if everyone believes Brett Higgins is dead." She smiled, looking deep into Allie's eyes, seeing her own love reflected there. She ran a hand across Allie's cheek. Allie was apparently also forgetting a cop named Randi McMartin who thought her lifelong ambition had been fulfilled two years ago when she attended Brett Higgins' funeral.

"But that still doesn't explain why we had to

leave. We were having a great time, weren't we?" Allie wrapped her arms around Brett's neck.

"Yes, we were, but I prefer not spending any more time around Tony Marzetti than is absolutely necessary."

"Tony Marzetti?"

Brett reached down and took Allie's hand as the waitress returned with their drinks. Clara's was a redesigned train depot, decorated with memorabilia and photographs. "Antonio Marzetti. He called himself Guy Franklin today. Rick introduced him to me one day at the theater. And I know I've seen that guy who walked up to him, but I just can't place him . . ."

"Chester Bombast?"

"My ass," Brett grumbled as she picked up a menu. "Nobody who looks like that is named Chester Bombast. Besides, I don't know anyone named that."

"So you're saying they both used code names?"

"Yeah, that's what I'm saying."

"So?"

"So their remarks sounded like code — kinda like 'the eagle flies at dawn' sorta thing."

"They were just discussing skiing!" Allie exclaimed, apparently frustrated with her lover's inability to give up the past and get on with life.

"Allison, Chester was not wearing Italian boots, and I doubt he's ever owned a pair of skis in his entire life. Plus, telemarking is something you do on cross-country skis, not downhill."

"Brett, we cannot run every time you think you hear a thunk in the night. You are out of the business now —"

"Do you remember that bombing with the carmakers a few years ago — in Detroit?"

"Yeah, they figured it had to do with the unions, because it was during a strike . . ."

"That was Tony."

"But they never figured out who did it!"

"It was Tony. And the other guy gave him cash and instructions today. If you had been really watching, you would have noticed the way he flipped through the smaller envelope — checking out his payment."

Allie looked across the table at her, then dropped her gaze to the menu. "The Chicken Kiev looks good, don't you think?"

Brett lifted Allie's chin so their eyes met. "You just have to believe me sometimes . . ."

"So what do you think we should do about it?" Allie asked after Brett paid the bill.

"Huh?" Brett replied, unable to follow her line of thought.

"What do you think we should do about Tony Marzetti?" Allie repeated as they headed out to the car.

Brett opened Allie's door for her. "I dunno. Something's gotta be going down, but there's no telling where. Even though the drop took place here, that's no indication as to the locale."

"So the only way to really do anything would be for you to admit to the police to being Brett Higgins, and say how you know him."

"And that'd be a guaranteed ride on the straight-to-hell express," Brett replied. "When I quit the life, about all I knew was that I'd never turn anyone in."

Allie nodded, understanding. Although they had never discussed it, it was always understood between them — in Brett's former occupation, turning people in was the worst of crimes. Everybody would be out to get her then — not even a relocation program could hide her well enough from those she turned in and those who worried she might.

Plus, getting involved with something like that would surely draw attention to Brett, and Allie couldn't help but think of her ex-lover Randi's unnatural obsession with Brett, even if Allie had finally convinced her that Brett hadn't killed her brother. Randi McMartin was a Detroit detective who thought Brett was dead and was a big part of the reason Brett was on the lam.

Allie breathed deeply of the cool night air, glad to be back in Michigan after a year in California, glad to once again be experiencing the coming spring, which you could feel in the air. She liked a state with changes in the weather — actual seasons. "You want to go for a walk down by the Capitol?" she suddenly asked as they climbed into the Explorer.

Brett smiled at her quizzically.

"It's just such a beautiful night."

Brett nodded and started the car, maneuvering out onto Lansing's myriad of one-way streets to head toward the Capitol. Allie moved a little closer to Brett and picked up her hand, holding it in her own. She loved Brett wholly and completely but sometimes worried that Brett missed her old life. Allie could tell that every once in a while Brett missed the fast-paced, exciting life she used to live, yet she wasn't quite the same woman she used to be. These days it was a bit easier bringing a smile to Brett's lips, getting her to open up and be excited about things like skiing — she had really enjoyed that, been truly happy about it. When they first met, it took an awful lot to get her to be simply happy about anything. Although Brett would probably never admit it, she had changed quite a bit in the past year.

Allie squeezed Brett's hand a little tighter and Brett wrapped her arm around Allie, pulling her in a little closer, as if she could sense Allie's thoughts as they drove wordlessly through the streets.

It was already much later than they had anticipated being in Lansing, but the night was beautiful and the streets were amazingly free and clear of traffic and pedestrians. They stood on the lawn of the Capitol, looking up at its lit dome, the distant chirping of early crickets providing the music of the night. The breeze was soft and a thousand stars twinkled above them. Allie ran her hand along Brett's cheek and let her thumb brush Brett's lips. A smile played across her lips as she looked deeply into her lover's eyes.

"You've got another gray hair," she teased, tugging playfully at the hair in question.

"Don't pull it!" Brett said. "Or else I'll get three more in its place!" These days Brett seemed to actually notice that she was pushing thirty. Allie hoped it wasn't just because she was six years younger than Brett that this change had occurred.

"The first time I ever saw you, I thought you looked like something dangerous, something from the other side."

"And now?"

"And now," Allie began, leaning back against the tall, wrought iron fence that surrounded the lawn of the Capitol, "now I know there's more to it. You're not quite what meets the eye."

"And is this a good thing or a bad thing?" Brett stepped forward so her body pressed against Allie's. They were such a perfect fit with Brett just an inch taller than her. Their bodies came together like the pieces of a jigsaw puzzle. Allie loved this sweet anticipation, knowing that in an hour or so she'd be making love with Brett, flesh against flesh with Brett inside of her. Suddenly, that hour or so seemed to stretch like an eternity before her.

"Definitely a good thing. If you were just any old big bad ass, I'd've dumped you a long time ago."

"Mmm, is that so?" Brett asked, burying her face in Allie's hair as she nibbled her neck, breathing deeply of the scent of Allie's perfume.

Allie moaned slightly but forced herself back to what she knew she had to say next. "And now I think you have to stay out of it — there's too much at risk for both of us. You need to focus on your new job. We need to focus on our new life."

"I hate to admit it, but I think you're right," Brett said. She held Allie tightly in her arms. She sighed. "I just hate admitting defeat."

"What are you thinking?" Allie whispered into her lover's ear a few minutes later.

Brett finally released her and pulled back to look into her eyes. "When I first saw you, I thought you were an angel dropped from heaven — and I still do." A smile touched her lips as she leaned forward to kiss Allie.

* * * * *

The sound of squealing tires made Brett look up just as a man ran past them. It was rather late in the day for a jogger. And he was wearing an expensive gray business suit with loafers and carrying a brief-case. He turned as he ran, as if watching for an unseen assailant. Suddenly a gunshot rang through the night air and he fell to the ground just a few feet from the two women.

"Get down!" Brett yelled as she pulled Allie off to the side while reaching for the gun that was always at her side — in the old days. "Shit!" She realized the gun wasn't there. Allie rolled to her knees and, crouching down, ran to where the man lay. Brett followed.

"It's just a phase," he slurred before he died. Allie felt for a pulse and found none. His black briefcase with a silver CJB monogram had broken its lock when it hit the ground and his diamond tie tack glittered in the moonlight.

"He's dead," she whispered to Brett. "And I really don't think it's just a phase."

Brett glanced down at his body. About fifty, with graying brown hair, he had a large hairless mole on his chin. He looked like he was just hitting middle-age spread but kept it well-hidden beneath expensive suits.

"Oh, fuck," Brett said, not liking this one bit. She stared a moment longer at the gaping chest wound that was pumping blood out onto the sidewalk, then jumped to her feet and took off toward Michigan Avenue — the direction the shot had come from. Allie followed her.

The full moon gave the briefest hints as to the whereabouts of the assailant as he dashed off the main thoroughfare. Brett saw his shadow dart down first one then another deserted side street as her feet pounded on the pavement. The streetlights here were mostly burned out once you got away from the Capitol, unless there just weren't any. Trash lined the streets she ran down, slowly gaining on the shooter.

He ducked into an alleyway ahead of her. She sprinted after him with Allie just behind her. A garbage can crashed down into her path and she leapt over it in hot pursuit. She saw a shadow leaping over a high fence ahead of her.

She hit the fence in a full run, throwing her foot up onto it, using her momentum to grab the top, where she pulled herself up and over. As she dropped to the ground on the other side, she saw a metallic gleam come from a streetlight reflecting off a gun. When she heard the bullets strike around her, she knew he was using a silencer and hoped Allie was proceeding with more caution than she had.

Brett rolled over to a dumpster, which she used as cover, and stood up. She saw a figure dash out of the alley and down the street. Allie dropped from the fence and ran up to her.

"That way," Brett whispered as she took off running out of the alley. It looked like the man they were following was also running out of breath and feeling the length of the chase. They hadn't even run a block, her heart pumping, when Brett heard a car bearing down on them from behind. She almost didn't see it because the headlights were off, but she threw an arm around Allie and jumped to the side — right into a row of trashcans.

The car roared by and Brett looked up just in time to miss getting any description of the car, its driver or license plate. She saw the brakelights briefly flash down the street as the driver, she presumed, picked up the person they had been following.

"Shit!" she yelled, getting to her feet and vainly looking in the direction the car had gone.

Allie stood up beside her and brushed herself off. "We should call the police," she said calmly, looking down the street.

"The police?" Brett asked, unable to relate to the fact that most people call the police when someone dies; she had spent years avoiding any interaction with the folks in blue.

"Brett, we have to."

Exhausted and out of breath, they stopped by Club 505, which was commonly called Five-O-Dive, to call 911 and then took the most direct route back to the body, covering the blocks at a fairly rapid pace. Even from a distance, they could see the flashing lights attesting to the quick response of the Lansing police department.

An officer gave them a quick once-over, eyeing their more than somewhat disheveled appearance. "Are you the two who called in the complaint?" he asked.

Brett instinctively turned from him, falling back into her old habits. She still didn't like talking with the police. There were only a few onlookers gathered around the scene, and soon a couple of them lost interest and headed off.

"Yes, we are," Allie replied quickly. "Do you have any idea who he is?"

"One thing at a time." He grimaced, pulling a notebook out of his breast pocket. "Hey, Ski!" he yelled over his shoulder. "I got 'em over here!"

The plainclothes detective named Ski turned out to

be a fairly good-looking woman with long, dark hair tied back in a ponytail, and a nice shape hidden under a black blazer, conservative white blouse and gray slacks.

"You the two who said you saw a murder?" she asked with a slight frown as she quickly sized them up. She seemed to pause with Allie. Brett had a brief, pleasant thought about Ski and Allie . . . and her.

"Yeah," Brett said before Allie could reply. "We saw some guy laid out right in front of us." She looked directly into Ski's hazel eyes, and noticed Ski hesitate before continuing.

"Could you describe this supposed incident to me?"

" 'Supposed incident?' " Brett asked with a grin. Leave it to cops to try to change one thing into something else.

Allie leapt to the detective's rescue with a full-blown account of the shooting, obviously knowing that Brett was about to slip into her smart-ass self. Brett watched the first officer, whose nameplate said Malone, take notes. She wandered over to where the police were packing up.

"What's goin' on?" Brett asked a cop nonchalantly, curious about who the poor sucker was.

"Ah, some crank called up and said there had been a murder," he replied with a shrug. "Then we get here and there ain't no body."

"Nobody, or no body?"

"No body," the cop replied. "Nothin' but a bit a blood, looks like somebody skinned their knee earlier skateboardin'. Crazy-ass kids, give 'em one nice day and they're climbing the walls and marching down the streets."

"Or maybe somebody dumped their cherry slushy all over," another cop added with a laugh.

"Are you sure there wasn't a body?" Brett persisted. What the hell happened?

"Listen, I know a dead body when I see one, and there ain't one here," he said, shaking his head. "Some punks got nothin' better to do with their time than call up the cops talkin' 'bout whatever they dream up."

Brett looked around. The body had been there less than a half-hour ago. Under the moonlight she could see some red on the pavement, but you could almost imagine it to be either from a skinned knee or some other minor injury. She flicked her Zippo and put her hand down over the bloodstain. The pavement was cool, from the night air, and wet — but not from blood. The surrounding sidewalk and some of the grass was wet too. Someone had washed the sidewalk. She fingered the wetness and sniffed. Yup, they had washed the sidewalk, with coffee they probably had in their car.

Stupid her, she had only seen the one fellow dash off, and she'd taken pursuit on the first glance she had. He no doubt had a partner who had ducked out of the way while she and Allie checked out the body and chased the first guy. Then the partner came, nabbed the body, cleaned up and went to pick up his friend. Stupid, stupid her. She should've known . . .

"I was a detective in Detroit — I wouldn't lie about something like this!" Allie was insisting when Brett returned.

"Listen," Ski said. "If there ain't no body, there ain't no murder. It's that simple. Show me a body and

I'll investigate a murder." Brett again found her gaze landing on Ski, who was just a bit shorter than she was, with soft features untouched by make-up. She was a femme trying to look rugged yet acceptable in a rough profession.

"Somebody washed the sidewalk over there," Brett said, indicating the area the police were vacating.

"It's wet. No tellin' what happened. Kid coulda dropped his pop."

"That would've happened during the day, when kids were around. It would've dried by now. And it's not pop, it's coffee."

Ski shrugged and pulled out a business card. Handing it to Allie she said, "If you think of anything else . . ."

"I'll give you a call," Allie replied, clearly unhappy with this turn of events.

Brett turned back to Ski, who was looking at her like someone suddenly reminded of a dream from a week ago. She grinned and winked in her direction.

Chapter Two

"How can a body up and disappear?" Allie asked Brett as they drove home.

"The shooter had an accomplice. While we chased him, his partner cleaned up then came to get him before we could."

Allie hadn't thought of anything like that, but Brett was probably right. "But who were they, who was he, and why'd they kill him?"

"It's not our problem, babe, after all, how can we solve a murder when there ain't no body?"

"We're a step ahead of the cops — at least we

know there's been a murder." She couldn't figure out how even Brett could be so casual about a murder. Especially one that had happened right in front of them.

Brett glanced over at Allie. "It seems like we're both having problems leaving our old lives behind," she remarked, referring to Allie's past as police officer/detective.

Allie sat back, watching the scenery fly by. She knew that both she and Brett were somewhat disconnected from most people's reality; most people would be more upset to see someone die right in front of them. Or maybe they were just fooling themselves and it had really affected them. Perhaps all of the day's events had affected them more than they were willing to admit, and all of it would, ultimately, surface again in a much more wicked way . . .

Worrying about it, though, wouldn't really help anything. Allie turned and looked at Brett, who was clearly lost deep in her own thoughts, so deep that she didn't notice Allie's gaze.

Allie thought gray hair was incredibly sexy on a woman, so although she teased Brett about it, she secretly loved it. All told, the two of them had been together for just over two years, but they had known each other for much longer than that. And all the while Allie had yearned for the feeling of Brett's hands on her, in her . . .

From the first moment she had ever laid eyes on Brett Higgins, she had felt a connection. She had been seventeen at the time, and even then she knew she had found someone special — someone who fit with her, could meld with her, yet challenge and stimulate her as well. Well, okay, she hadn't immediately been conscious of all those things, because she was too busy fantasizing how she would go about seducing this incredibly dangerous-looking woman, but she had forced herself up out of her shell because she hadn't wanted to risk losing her.

Even when they were separated, a separation brought about when Allie realized Brett had been cheating on her, Allie couldn't stop thinking about her. She had tried dating, but nobody could match up to her. Nobody else, not even Randi, who said she loved Allie, looked at her the way Brett did: eyes full of passion, love and promise.

She glanced again at Brett's profile, remembering what Brett had once said about their being soulmates, and knew again, as if she were just realizing it, although she had known it for years, just how right that phrase was.

She suddenly realized that tonight's events had left her filled with energy and excitement. She had loved the thrill of the chase, the danger of being shot at, the trauma of being hit with a mystery, although her wiser side told her they couldn't follow up on it.

She glanced over at Brett's thick, graying black hair, her solemn jaw and stern mouth. She was mulling over something, but Allie couldn't help but think of the powerful arms hidden beneath the black leather jacket, the well-defined collarbone revealed by her open-necked shirt, the strong hands casually draped on the steering wheel . . . and of what those hands could do to her, those hands and those lips . . .

She wanted Brett but knew this was not the time. It was about an hour's drive from Lansing to their home in Alma.

They drove up to their neat little two-story house

in "Little Scotland," Alma, Michigan. The house was in Allie's name. Brett's new identity didn't have much of a real past associated with it. Because Allie didn't need to run from anybody she didn't need to change her name. Of course, this was irrelevant since they had bought the house privately, with cash, for less than a quarter of what Allie had sold her parents' house in Sterling Heights for after their death.

Brett flipped on the light switch and headed straight to the phone. It was after midnight, but she knew Frankie kept hours as strange as hers and she knew what she had seen tonight was too organized to be a random killing. She wanted to know what was going on — after all, that was one of her fortés, having knowledge in advance so she could make good decisions.

"Yeah," Frankie said, answering on the third ring. He didn't like answering machines.

"Heya, Frankie. I got a problem and I was hoping you might know something about it." The two of them had been through a lot together and had an unspoken vow to be there for each other. They had taken over their boss Rick's business when Rick had been killed, and it was Frankie who had helped Brett create the new identity of Samantha Peterson.

When Allie walked back into Brett's life, Frankie knew Brett was thinking of retiring from the scene. Of course, at that time, they didn't realize Allie was working undercover with Detroit's special organized crime team, along with Randi McMartin. Although Randi wanted to get Brett as part of her commitment to truth, justice and the American way, she also wanted Brett because she thought Brett had killed her brother. Brett hadn't, but she had been involved in Daniel's death.

One stormy night a year and a half ago, Randi had tried to set a trap to catch Brett. At that time, Randi had been dating Allie as well, but she was willing to use Allie to get Brett. That night Allie chased Brett onto the roof of the Paradise Theatre, the home base for Brett and Frankie's operations, and had shot and killed someone. Allie thought she had killed Brett, and the body had been so mutilated by the shooting and the fire that broke out that everyone assumed it was Brett, but it wasn't. It was a dancer named Kirsten Moore, who was then buried in a grave with Brett Higgins' name on it.

Allie quit the police force on the day Kirsten was buried, but she didn't learn until after the funeral that Brett was still alive.

Now, the only two people in the world who knew who Brett was and that she was still alive were Frankie and Allie.

"So what's goin' on?" Frankie asked, bringing Brett back to the present.

"Let's just say it was a busy day." Brett quickly recounted the day's events, from seeing the drop with Tony and the other guy, whom she knew from somewhere, to seeing the man killed in front of them.

"Brett. It's none of your business now. Just report it to the cops."

"Y'know I can't tell them about Tony, and as for that poor son-of-a-bitch, well, he disappeared."

"Whaddya mean he disappeared?"

"When we got back his body was gone." Brett

knew by Frankie's pause that he was thinking the same thing she was — that a random killer wouldn't have gone to the trouble of getting rid of the body. "Frankie, I don't like this. We both know bodyies don't just up and disappear. I want to know who the hell he was, who did him and why. Ya got any info?"

"I can check into it." He paused again. "Brett, be careful. You can't afford to get caught up in this sort of shit."

"Fuck, Frankie, y'know my luck. This sorta shit just don't happen without someone lookin' at me." She leaned back on the sofa and stared at the ceiling. "So what else has been going on?"

Frankie chuckled. It felt good to hear his familiar laugh, bringing back all the good times they had had together. He said, "You just won't believe this one. Your old pal Jack O'Rourke wants me to go into business with him."

Detroit's mafia, although they no longer referred to themselves as such, preferring instead terms such as *partners*, *mob* or *the outfit*, had just been lassoed in the past few years, with several kingpins going to jail. But Detroit's operations had never gained the reputation or power of those in cities such as New York or Chicago, and that left room for smaller operators. Rick DeSilva, Frankie's and Brett's beloved old boss, had been the largest of these, dealing mostly with drug trafficking and pornography.

Jack O'Rourke's operation was just slightly smaller than Rick's, but he apparently saw not only the fall of the kingpins, but also Rick's and Brett's deaths as a means to expand his holdings. He had always been involved with drugs, racketeering, bookmaking and coercement, but apparently wanted to add a few more things to his repertoire.

He had approached Frankie about going into business together, or buying Frankie out, but Frankie wouldn't have anything to do with it. Both Brett and Frankie knew Jack's offer would be Frankie's most profitable outlet, because Frankie didn't have Brett's business sensibilities or knowledge, but Frankie held grudges. The particular grudge he had against Jack was that a few years ago Jack had tried to have Brett offed.

One of the many things Brett loved about Frankie was his loyalty.

When Brett finally hung up the phone an hour later, she was almost surprised to find Allie still awake, even though Allie had been in the same room she was the entire time, reading a book.

"You miss it, don't you?" Allie asked, uncurling herself from her chair.

"Sometimes, yeah. It was exciting, an adventure." Brett noticed how differently she spoke, depending on whom she was talking with.

"Mmm, and our life together isn't?' Allie asked, sitting next to Brett. She pulled Brett around to gently massage her back and shoulders. "You need to let it go, honey. You don't need to worry every time something happens around you."

Her hands felt so good. "I can't help it. I just get these feelings, and it's not just paranoia."

"Let it go, baby, let it go." Brett was now lying on the sofa, with Allie straddling her hips. The only light in the room was from the reading lamp Allie had been using. The light perfume of incense filled the air. Brett hadn't realized how tense she had gotten over the day's events until she felt Allie's tender, knowing hands work her muscles. She became aware of Allie's lips on her neck.

"It'll be okay, baby," Allie was murmuring in her ear.

Brett rolled over under Allie, looking up at her graceful features, her heart swelling with love for this woman who knew her so well. No one else could ever understand her needs and wants so well, not even herself.

She sat up, pulling Allie into her arms, and kissed her full on the lips. When Allie's mouth opened, Brett gently entered her, their tongues meeting in warmth while Allie's perfume danced over Brett's senses. Brett ran her hands down Allie's back, gradually moving up under Allie's shirt. She suddenly needed to be closer, to break down barriers between them.

Allie stood and led her upstairs to their bedroom. In the moonlit room they slowly undressed each other, Brett unable to touch Allie enough. Allie laid Brett down on the bed, her naked flesh warm on Brett's.

Brett enjoyed Allie's curves, the supple softness of her breasts, the scent of her arousal. She rolled Allie onto her back and worked her way down her body, over the soft skin of her throat, to hardened nipples, which she teased back and forth between her teeth, over her slender belly, taking her time to play her tongue over Allie's navel ring.

She then moved down to Allie's feet, first one and then the other, sucking at her toes before kissing and licking her way up lightly muscled calves and thighs. She spread Allie's legs, sitting up between them and running her hands down over her stomach into the thick patch of blond hair before burying herself in Allie's wetness.

She needed to be inside Allie, and Brett always took what she needed.

Allie moaned at Brett's entrance, first one finger, then another, until her entire fist was buried inside her. Brett loved feeling Allie open up for her, expand to take her in. She loved moving her fist around, feeling so much a part of the woman she loved, and loved feeling Allie's muscles contract and tighten around her when she came in a maelstrom of tossing and pitching.

Afterward, when they lay in each other's arms, Allie on the verge of sleep, Brett whispered softly into her ear, "I love you."

Adrenaline pumped through her system . . .

She was a child, her faithful teddy bear Boo Boo Bearski clutched in her arms while her father hit her and kicked her and picked her up. She was flying through the air only to be stopped by a wall. She fell to the floor and could barely focus before another attack began, this time with her brothers joining in, her mother standing helplessly to the side . . .

Then she was a full-grown woman . . .

And they were right behind her as her heart pumped in her chest and the night closed in around her like the shroud of death. She heard the roar of their guns as she turned to shoot back at them, tires squealing in the darkness. She had to get away, get away before they could catch her, before they could hurt her . . .

There was the shattering of glass and she was on her feet, moving stealthily through the shadows, stalking him as he hunted her and hers. She went into a dive, exposing herself, the floor racing up at her as she rolled to land on her knees, her gun in her hands as she aimed right between his eyes, the recoil barely touching her as the man collapsed mere feet from her, his head a bloody mess . . .

The man lay almost unconscious from pain on the floor before her, and she felt a sickening thud reverberate through her arm as the butt of her gun met with his solid skull and blood splashed from his head onto the sleeve of her blazer . . .

And Frankie was there suddenly, helping her move the men. *Friends help friends move, real friends help friends move bodies.* She was telling her lover, Storm, not to let anyone in until they returned. Then they were driving over the icy roads until they reached the abandoned warehouse. Filled with loathing and disgust, she watched Frankie take aim and fire dead-on at the man whose face she had crumpled earlier, who was now lying on the ground in front of him . . .

It was months later. She was in the pouring rain, with thunder and lightning competing with the flashing red of police lights. She felt the weight of her gun as she aimed at the dim form not twenty feet away. Had she been a religious woman, she would have prayed as she pulled the trigger.

The blare of the gun reverberated off the buildings, rolled with the thunder. Unharmed, the figure turned toward her. Allie. She hoisted the gun again, wiped the rain out of her eyes and aimed with even more care, wishing that she could be dead herself, but knowing she had to get Allie to shoot at her, knowing, as the sirens blared, as the red and blue lights reflected off each pellet of rain, that it was the only solution, the only way out . . .

She wished she could say goodbye to Frankie.

Brett awoke with a start. It took her a few moments to realize she was safe at home, in her bed, with Allie beside her. She curled up spoonlike behind Allie, but the images from the dream came back, the gunfire ringing in her ears like the backbeat to the song of her life, the danger and excitement pumping adrenaline back into her system, a feeling she had almost forgotten existed.

Brett rolled onto her back, away from Allie, and stared at the ceiling. She couldn't stop thinking of herself as Brett Higgins, although that was a bit of her past that was best left dead. There were too many people far too happy to see Brett Higgins dead and buried, too many people with too many grudges against her. But she couldn't see herself at a desk job for the rest of her life, trapped by a time clock into doing mind-numbing repetitive work she hated. She needed to be active, to live on the wild side, to be challenged both mentally and physically.

She crept out of bed, trying not to wake Allie, then slipped on her robe and picked up the clothes she had worn earlier. Downstairs, she threw the pants and blazer into the trash. Earlier in the evening, on their drive back from Lansing, she had noticed blood splotches on them. Even now, she felt disgust at the sight she had witnessed, although she could barely believe that just a few years ago spilt blood had been a big part of her life — blood let loose either through injury or death. She had lost more than a little blood herself along the way and knew she was lucky to still be alive.

She poured herself a scotch on the rocks and sat looking out the window at the night sky flooded with stars, thinking about all the deaths she'd witnessed in her lifetime . . . And all the women she'd had, she silently added.

She loved Allie, and never wanted to lose her again, but sometimes she missed the thrill of the chase, the excitement of the conquest, the dance of flirtation. In some ways it seemed that she was doomed to be a free spirit, that she'd never be happy with a staid, stable, predictable life.

She went into her den and from her desk pulled out her hand-crafted, long-throated Savinelli pipe, with its long, slender curves that she enjoyed running her fingers over. She liked the deeply tanned, smooth, polished wood of the bowl, liked cupping it in her hand while she gently puffed on it. It was an Italian pipe, and although the best pipes were supposed to be the Dunhills, she liked this one the best because Frankie had given it to her many years ago, when they still worked together. It reminded her of him, and how he and Rick DeSilva had taught her to enjoy fine scotch, pipes and cigars.

Brett took a leather packet from the drawer, dipping the pipe into it so she could gently fill it, tamp it, fill it again and tamp it down again. She'd finally found a local tobacconist who was able to mix her special blend. Although several different types of tobacco were acceptable, she preferred her own blend, and Rick had taught her that it was best to only smoke one type of tobacco in each pipe because the flavor would slowly soak into the wood, making each consecutive smoke a little fuller.

She rotated the flame from her Zippo over the bowl while inhaling. She kept the Zippo close at hand in case the pipe went out, as it tended to do at first.

The pipe reminded her of the past, the best parts of the past, the times when she was at her finest. She hoped those days weren't forever gone. Although she never once regretted what she had done, she knew she couldn't go back.

She swiveled her chair around so she could see the picture of Allie she had hung on the wall. Allie had brought her back to life, had given her a fresh start. Whatever had happened to the woman who had wanted to succeed, to be somebody? It was true, she hadn't had a name for the first five years of her life, because her parents hadn't felt like giving her one, and yes, she still wanted to go back and show her family and all her other tormentors just who the hell she was. But now, especially because of one cop, she would never see that day. One cop who had wanted her badly enough to make her risk it all and make a choice.

For just over a year, she'd been Samantha Peterson, and all the old debts lay in the name of Brett Higgins. Only Madeline, their next-door neighbor, Frankie and Allie called her Brett now. Anyone who asked about this was told her name was Samantha Brett Peterson, and it had been an old childhood nickname.

Although Allie had known her for seven years, Frankie was the one who knew her not only the longest but also the best. Ever since they had met, they had been there for each other, doing whatever needed to be done, including killing.

Brett suddenly realized she couldn't imagine ever killing anyone again. Yes, earlier that night her first reaction had been to catch the murderer so that there was no way she could be blamed for the killing, but she also knew she wanted to see justice done. No one deserved to be shot in the back like that man had been. Killed outright in cold blood.

It was true: her old life, with all that it had been and all that she had accomplished, was now a childhood nickname.

Chapter Three

It was a bright, clear April morning. Michigan weather had always been known for its fickleness, but the past few years had been even more extreme than before, with global warming and El Niño showing their power by making the days unseasonably warm and sunny.

Unfortunately, it was also a Monday, Brett's first day of work at her new job, and she knew something was up even before she entered the building. She wished she could say her years of experience in sniffing out and evading the police made her realize this, but in truth it was the six police cars and one ambulance that clued her in.

There were about three dozen different businesses located in the 12-story office building in downtown Lansing, but when the elevator stopped at the ninth floor, which was occupied solely by BB&B Advertising, the four policemen who rode up with her got off there as well.

The place was in an uproar, with uniformed and plainclothes police scurrying around like maggots on a corpse. The middle-aged female receptionist who had greeted Brett during her interviews with cool, calm and poise now had a panicked look frozen on her face while she frantically answered phone calls and quickly threw them into the dungeons of hold and voice mail.

Brett determined that her best course of action would be to find either the personnel director or any of the people who had interviewed her. As she went through the austere halls, the floors padded with an industrial tan carpeting, the walls covered in a textured off-white wallpaper decorated with occasional flares of orange and green, she felt a definite difference in the atmosphere. On her prior visits, the place had a charged energy about it; people rushed about with important work to do and deadlines to meet. Now, however, there was still an energy, but it was frenetic and aimless. People hovered behind half-closed doors. Phones rang and went unanswered. There was a conspiratorial hum of whispers and murmurs.

As she rounded the bend, still seeking a familiar face or office, she realized she had found the eye of the storm: a large group of people gathered near a corner office. Brett pushed toward the front of the crowd, heedless of the uniformed police barring the way, and looked inside. The appointed office, with its Ethan Allen desk and upholstered chairs belonging to someone high up in the company, was in disarray. Pictures hung askew on walls, books were tossed from their mahogany shelves, drawers were emptied onto the floor, framed family photos were strewn carelessly about, and Brett noticed a familiar black briefcase with a broken lock and silver CJB monogram lying within the ruins.

Just behind the desk two men were placing a gray-suited body into a heavy black bag. There was a large patch of red spread across his chest, radiating outward from a gaping hole. Brett stared into the face of the corpse, with its large hairless chin mole, hair that was once brown but was now almost entirely gray and memorized every feature of the face. She noted the Italian-cut, double-breasted gray suit and diamond tie-tack as the bag was zipped up and over the entire body. As the attendants lugged the bag onto a stretcher and brought it out through the crowd, she felt a chill. It was the man she had seen killed at the Capitol.

Stunned, Brett turned to leave only to find herself staring into the hazel eyes of the same detective from Saturday night. Ski looked back at her, those eyes alert and penetrating.

Brett quickly darted down the hall in search of Personnel, hoping Ski hadn't recognized her, but knowing she had.

* * * * *

Alexandra Perkins, the personnel director who had hired her, was a bleached blond, shrewish, anorexic woman with sharp, thin features and an overbite.

"This will be your office," she said, leading Brett into a small room with a desk, a computer, a few chairs, a filing cabinet and a bookshelf loaded with a wide array of texts and tomes. The nameplate on the door read *Samantha Peterson, Media Planner/Buyer*.

When Brett and Allie discussed finding a new profession for Brett they immediately decided upon business — after all, Brett did have a degree in it from Michigan State University. From there, she quickly shunned the types of business, such as sales, that would require her to wear a skirt and pumps. They finally thought of advertising, which they had heard was far less prone to glass ceilings and closed-mindedness than other jobs. Plus, Brett figured, it seemed intriguing and challenging enough to possibly hold her interest. It was worth a try, especially when it turned out that their friend and neighbor, Madeline Jameson, had a few contacts at BB&B, a Lansing ad agency, and was able to arrange an interview for Brett. Of course, what Madeline didn't know was that Brett had created her entire résumé from the internet, using it to create a small base of agencies and clients she had worked for.

Brett hadn't had to think twice about putting aside any ambitions toward the creative end of the business, knowing she had neither the talent nor the inventive mind required for copywriting, art direction, or even production. That left account work or media. Account work posed too high a risk of having to dress nicely, and although she could sell crates of videos and sex toys to store owners all over Detroit, she had no idea how to sell something as seemingly intangible as an ad agency's services.

Thus she ended up in media. Now she just had to bluff her way through the first week or two while she figured everything out and hope that no one would ever realize that her entire résumé was a lie. At least she had taken a few marketing and advertising courses in college so she could bluff through a lot of the terminology, and she had, after all, been somewhat of a sales/business person in her last position, though she could hardly list her life of crime on her résumé.

"You're in luck," Alexandra was saying. "It appears you even have a stapler." She glanced up at Brett. "Anyway . . . I have to admit that, to be honest, I'm really not that sure of anybody's job security around here at this moment."

"What do you mean by that?"

"Well, you know that was Chuck they found . . ."

"Chuck?"

"Chuck Bertram. He was the president and owner." Alexandra began to flutter nervously about the office, checking the supplies, switching on the computer and straightening chairs and books. Brett read this as a sign that she wanted to discuss the incident with someone, anyone.

"What about the other two Bs?" Brett inquired, referring to the name of the company.

"Well, one is his wife, Sara Bertram, a real wench. Chuck was always the nicer of the two." She perched on the edge of the desk, her brow furrowed in thought. "As for the third B, well, I just don't know.

Our little joke around here," she confided, "is that BB&B actually stands for Baffled, Bewildered and Bemused."

Brett let out the obligatory chuckle.

"I just don't know what I'll do if they close this place down, though. I've been here for ten years now and the job market just isn't what it used to be."

"I'm sure his wife will keep the place open. I mean, from the looks of it, the place is doing pretty good."

"From the looks of it, sure . . ." She paused, then shook her head, as if suddenly remembering her professionalism. "I'm sorry, I think you remind me of my priest when I was growing up. I shouldn't be going on and on, I'm just not myself today . . ."

"For good reason," Brett assured her, wondering if what she meant was that the agency only looked as if it was doing well.

"I'm sure everything will be just fine," Alexandra twittered before she bustled off.

Brett glanced at her watch. It was just after eleven. A quick investigation of the department showed that all the other media people were elsewhere, so she could either spend some time searching her own office and attempting to learn something about her new job, or she could roam BB&B in search of further information. One glance at the loaded bookshelf sent her off to stalk the halls, but she was quickly intercepted by Richard Pettibone, the gray-haired, gruff-looking media director.

"Sam! There you are. Alex said she left you in your office — I completely forgot you were starting today, what with all the ruckus about the murder and all."

"It's understandable," Brett remarked, suddenly realizing that no one she had seen or spoken with seemed particularly upset over Chuck's death.

"I'd take you around and introduce you to everybody, but that detective woman wants us all in the conference room, as if I have time for any of this nonsense, especially if we're supposed to keep this place running for Sara."

Brett allowed herself to be led to the conference room while Richard — or Dick, as everybody called him — rattled on about all the different projects the media department was involved in and how she would fit into their team.

"If I know Alex," Dick was saying, "she's got you quite worried about your position with us, but I wouldn't worry. We've got quite a lot going on, and it was really Sara who ran the agency anyway. Chuck was your typical account man, all show and no action."

Uh-oh. Brett hadn't even considered office politics when she decided to accept this position. She wasn't used to having to play sides when dealing with things as ludicrously simple as facts and figures. People could make so little into so much just to keep their imaginations running rampant.

The conference room was packed with the fifty or so employees of BB&B, plus Ski and a man who was apparently her partner. Looking as if they'd already had a long day in their rumpled blazers and slacks, the detectives stood at the front of the room. Brett recognized the bulges of guns under the blazers and could empathize with their opened collars. It was a real bugger to be trapped in a blazer because you didn't want anyone to know you were carrying.

Ski again met her eyes, going so far as to boldly look her up and down. A frown crossed her face. It was obvious she was trying to place Brett, and Brett could only hope it was merely from Saturday night.

Brett threw on her cockiest attitude and winked at her. Ski immediately turned away, apparently somewhat abashed by the brazen gesture.

Next to Ski's partner was a flashy blond who wore a dark blue business suit with a white silk blouse and pumps. She had Barbra Streisand's nose and a helmet of hair. Brett had to admit she was a real knock-out, but, as the woman blotted her face with a Kleenex, Brett also noticed that her bright red fingernails were surprisingly short.

Brett looked futilely around for a seat and ended up standing in the doorway.

The blond exchanged a few more words with Ski's partner, then turned to the room. "Settle down, everybody. We'll try to make this as quick as possible." She blotted her eyes again, then turned her back to blow her nose. Brett remembered what Alexandra said earlier and decided this had to be Chuck's wife, Sara. She seemed a bit more upset than everyone else, but then again, how many people really knew their boss well enough to cry at the funeral, especially when job security was at stake. "To begin with," Sara continued, "I just want to assure everybody that I will do everything in my power to ensure that things remain business as usual here at BB&B." Another pause for grief. "Until we know more, I expect everybody to keep on as if nothing had happened. I'm sure Chuck —" She took a deep breath. "Would want it that way . . . Please . . . Please excuse me . . ." She rushed toward the door in a massive emotional outpouring. She bumped into Brett, who was still standing in the doorway, on her way out. She looked up into Brett's eyes for just a moment, and Brett felt an immediate connection.

Brett expected someone to go comfort her, but no one did. Everyone merely looked at one another, waiting for someone else to do it. A murmur arose as they all began talking at once, some voices raised in concern, although no one moved.

"Excuse me," Ski said. "I'm detective Joan Lemanski and this is my partner Paul Graves . . ."

That was all Brett heard as she left the room in search of Sara.

She found Sara huddled on the couch in her office, which was the corner office at the opposite end of the building from Chuck's, around the corner and down the hall from her own. She looked surprised when Brett knocked then entered the room. She had the deepest brown eyes Brett had ever seen. They reminded Brett of something, though she couldn't quite place what. A sardonic half-smile crossed Sara's full lips. "You must be new here."

"Just tell me if I'm out of bounds — I know I don't really know you and all . . ." Brett suddenly remembered that she was not good around death. Well, okay, she was fine around death per se; it was trying to comfort the survivors that gave her problems. Of course, that wasn't the real issue here. Brett had followed her partly because she had an excuse to, partly out of curiosity, and partly to avoid Ski.

"I'm Sara," she said, patting the couch next to her.

"Sam, Sam Peterson. I'm in media," Brett explained as she sat down, throwing her arm casually along the back of the couch as she turned to face Sara.

Sara dropped her pumps to the floor and curled her legs up under her as she leaned against the arm of the leather sofa, facing Brett. The movement caused her navy skirt to hike a bit farther up her shapely thighs. "I would've thought you'd be an account type — you have a certain demeanor, a confidence about you, if you don't mind my saying so," she finished, looking into Brett's eyes. Her mascara had begun to run, even though she had temporarily stopped crying. There was a box of tissues on the couch next to her, and she clutched one in her hand.

"You are the boss and all."

"Yeah, I guess this is all mine now. It's funny, you work every day with people, and you don't realize until a time like this just how disliked you are."

"Oh, I don't think . . ."

"It won't take you long to learn all sorts of interesting nicknames for me, I'm sure. I knew there was some tension, but . . ."

Brett felt a need to comfort Sara. She laid her hand on her shoulder. "People just act funny around death."

Sara put her hand on top of Brett's. It was cool and dry and soft. "No," she said with a chuckle. "They just don't like me. And you'd better watch out or else you'll get the reputation of a brown-noser."

"I've never been someone to give a rat's ass about what anyone thinks of me."

Sara looked deep in her eyes, then pulled Brett's hand down to her lap, where she held it within her own. "Why do I know that's the truth?" she asked, as she ran her thumbs up and down the back of Brett's hand. It could've been an intimate gesture, but Brett had the feeling her hand had merely replaced the tissue as Sara's security blanket.

Brett studied Sara's pearl necklace and remembered once hearing that pearls said, "Trust me." Brett judged that she was somewhere in her mid-thirties and would probably remain beautiful until she died. The laugh lines on her face bespoke someone who enjoyed life.

"Dick likes you," Brett said.

Sara smiled at this. "Yes, he would. Chuck and I often had to play good cop/bad cop around here, and since Chuck was the more easygoing of us . . ." She shrugged as a tear wound its way down her cheek, further streaking her mascara.

"You got to be the bad guy, keeping people in line," Brett said, reaching for a tissue to wipe Sara's face.

Sara allowed Brett to clean her face. "Dick's been around quite a while, and he and Chuck never quite hit it off. I'm afraid he's expecting more of me than I can provide." She shook her head slightly before leaning it on the back of the couch, and Brett's arm. "I just hope I don't disappoint him and everybody else who works here."

"Dick doesn't seem the sort to buy a lightshow. I'm sure his confidence is well-placed."

"I just . . . Damnit, I keep thinking, 'What would Chuck say if he were here?' He hasn't even been gone more than a couple of days, and I already miss him like hell." She paused, sitting up to again face Brett. "I was worried when he didn't show up Saturday night, but I knew he had a meeting down in Detroit that might've lasted late enough for him to spend the night there. I knew it was only logical for him to get a hotel room, even though it was so unlike him to do that without calling me. I knew something was wrong when he didn't show up yesterday at all and I still hadn't heard from him . . ." The tears were now running freely down over her carefully made-up face. Brett didn't think she needed the make-up at all to be beautiful. She also knew the denial, the self-loathing and recriminations Sara was going through.

"There's nothing you could've done," Brett said, inching closer to Sara. She wanted to comfort her, but she didn't know her, and she was her new boss after all.

"But what was he doing *here*?"

Brett recognized the pain in Sara's eyes, recognized it as the same pain she had been through years before. She reached forward and pulled Sara into her arms, gently smoothing back her hair and cooing soothing words while the woman sobbed against her.

Sara had finally calmed down and finished sniffling against Brett's sleeve, relaxing for a moment in Brett's arms before returning to her attempt at a business-as-usual persona when the door opened.

"We'll start . . ." Ski trailed off as she saw the tableau spread in front of her. "The questioning after lunch," she finished after a moment. Sara sat up and put her pumps back on as Brett leisurely turned to face Ski. She knew bolting would only make her look all the more guilty, as if she were hiding something. If only Sara hadn't stopped crying, if only this weren't her first day.

"I don't believe we've met," Ski said, walking into the room and looking at Brett.

"Detective Lemanski, this is Sam Peterson. Sam just started with us . . ."

"Today, today's my first day," Brett said, standing and looking at Ski, extending her hand with a grin. "Pleased to meet you."

Realization suddenly crossed Ski's face. "Saturday night," she said. "You were the woman from Saturday night," she said, pointing at Brett.

"Yeah, that was me, the woman with no body."

"Well, I'm glad to see you've found it," Sara said, looking Brett up and down.

"Have you now?" Ski asked.

Brett paused before she answered, carefully considering the repercussions of her answer. "You wouldn't believe me the other night, so why should I expect anything different now?"

"A smart ass, huh? You know I could take you in for withholding evidence."

"Evidence? I don't have any evidence. All I have is a story that nobody believed."

"Since you missed the little gathering in the conference room, I'll fill you in. My partner and I will be questioning everybody at the agency — including you."

"Detective," Sara interjected, "Sam just started with us, I'm sure she won't know —"

"I'll see you in the conference room in five minutes," Ski told Brett.

Chapter Four

"I thought we were gonna wait till after lunch to start the interviews," Brett heard a man say. It would have to be Ski's partner, Paul Graves, who seemed a little too aptly named for his profession.

Brett paused outside the conference room, waiting for more.

"We were," Ski replied. "But then I walked in on Sam Peterson having an intimate little tête-à-tête with Sara Bertram." Her voice was as cold as the frozen ground in a Michigan cemetery in winter. But Brett reminded herself of the passion that seemed just below the surface with the hard-nosed detective — real feelings no doubt submerged by fear. Brett knew the type well. Neither the criminals nor her male co-workers would see anything but the stereotypical dyke cop — that was, if Ski even knew she was a dyke.

"So you think the grieving little widow has a lover on the side?" Paul said. A shuffling of papers. "I don't see a Sam Peterson on here."

"She just started today."

"She?"

"Yes, she."

"Sara doesn't strike me as that sort."

Ski paused. "Trust me on this one. I just get a feeling from both of them. I don't think it was mere comfort Peterson was giving Sara back there."

Brett knew she'd better get in there before they came looking for her. When she entered the room carrying a cup of coffee and a pack of cigarettes, Ski glanced at her watch. Brett sat down, lit a cigarette, leaned back in her chair, propped her feet up on the conference table and grinned.

"I'd apologize for being late except, if you had let me get a word in, I would've told you it would take me longer than five minutes to find a pack of cigarettes."

"And you needed one," Ski said, looking away from Brett.

"I always like to smoke when being interrogated by the police."

"And this happens often?"

"Twice in three days now."

"I didn't notice you smoking Saturday night."

"That doesn't mean I didn't want one," Brett said, flashing her best shit-ass grin.

Ski leaned over the table. "I'd ask you what you were doing that night, but I already know that. At least, for part of the night."

Brett pushed her hand back through her hair and winked at Ski, who colored slightly. She knew she should behave, but cops made her defensive, and she didn't like being defensive. "Allie and I went skiing at Alpine Valley that day. We stopped by Clara's in Lansing for dinner and, because it was such a nice night, decided to go for a walk by the Capitol."

"Clara's?" Paul asked, jotting notes. He obviously intended to check out her alibi.

"Yes, I did."

"Isn't it a little late in the season for skiing?" Ski asked.

Brett glanced at the ceiling. Now she was supposed to justify wanting one more day out on the slopes, even if they were in substandard condition?

"Couldn't've been much snow out there," Ski continued, moving in on Brett.

"Why don't we cut the crap now? Did I kill Chuck Bertram? No. Was that Chuck Bertram I saw killed Saturday night? Yes." She stood up and approached Ski, who stood to her full height, trying to meet Brett eye to eye. "Am I having an affair with Sara Bertram? No. What was my relationship with the deceased and his wife? Never met Chuck, not formally really, just saw him killed. As for Sara — never met her until today."

"So you often hold hands with strangers?" Ski said.

"No one should be left alone in pain."

"And who hired you into the company?"

"Alexandra Perkins, the personnel director."

"So you didn't interview with Sara or Chuck?"

"No. I already said I hadn't met them."

"You just interviewed with Perkins?"

"And Dick Pettibone, the media director, and two media supervisors."

"And they can corroborate this?"

"Yes."

"How are you so sure it was Bertram you saw killed?"

"Same suit, tie tack, briefcase. Same face, down to the mole on his chin —"

"You noticed all of this even though it was dark out?" Paul said. He looked like he'd been watching tennis, his head going back and forth as the two women volleyed.

"You notice a lot at a time like that, and it just doesn't leave you. You remember that face."

"You've seen a lot of people killed?" Ski asked.

Brett paused, taken aback. "Yes," she finally said. "On TV. It's quite a different experience in real life." Ski didn't blink. She had noticed the pause. "Look, even you gotta admit it would be way stupid of me to start work today if I just offed Chuck Saturday night . . ." Did she really just say *offed*? Paul and Ski continued to watch her. "Furthermore" — she straightened her tie and jacket lapels —"I don't have a motive or opportunity. You will discover this once you check my alibi."

Ski again waited for her to continue. When she didn't she said, "Where do you come from, originally?"

Brett knew she was thinking she did have a

motive if she was having an affair with Sara. "I live in Alma."

"I said originally — as in, where were you born?"

"Originally?" Brett repeated. She leaned back against the table. "Originally I come from somewhere else."

"Where?"

"You're the detective. Figure it out yourself." She looked at her watch. "If you need anyone to verify my whereabouts Saturday, day or night, you can talk with my *roommate*, Allison Sullivan. You've already met her. As for now, I need to grab some lunch before getting back to work." She needed time to think. She had to get out of here before she let herself slip any further.

"I'm not through with you yet."

Brett stopped at the door. "Yes, you are. I'm leaving now."

Paul stepped forward. "Any cooperation you show at this time —"

"Yeah, I know," Brett interrupted. "Come talk to me later, because right now you're just cruisin' the bar, and it's nowhere near last call yet . . . And in fact," she continued, slowly looking Paul and Ski up and down, "you're in the wrong bar, 'cause what you're lookin' for ain't even here." She grinned, even though she knew she was in deep shit. The last thing she needed right now was to be a suspect in a murder investigation.

Brett went out to lunch and tried to get in touch with Allie on her cellular phone while waiting in the drive-through at a nearby fast-food restaurant. When

Allie didn't answer, she didn't leave a message because she didn't want Allie calling her back at work about this.

After lunch she spent the afternoon perusing the various tomes on her bookshelf. One series contained information on all the different magazine, newspaper, radio station, direct mail, television and outdoor advertising venues in the U.S. Another set noted magazine readership demographics. The list of reference books went on. This job looked like it might be a touch more difficult than she originally anticipated — especially since she couldn't make head or tail of some of the books.

Around three, Dick took her around to introduce her to everyone, including the media assistants, but aside from that, everyone was still in such a tizzy that it seemed as if they all forgot her existence, so she was pretty much left to her own devices, which for a while consisted of trying to perfect the design of a paper airplane.

She knew she had to do something but couldn't quite decide what. She thought about leaving and not coming back, but she didn't want to have to go on the lam again for crimes she didn't commit.

The police continued their investigation, with patrolmen taking statements from lesser employees, and Ski and Paul interviewing key personnel themselves in the conference room, starting with Sara Bertram.

While studying, Brett kept getting coffee from the kitchen so she could watch the police carefully, finally determining that they were using an office two doors down from Sara's as their base. At 4:30 Brett saw Sara leave, so at 4:45, when Paul and Ski closed themselves into their office, she slipped into Sara's office and closed the door. She climbed onto the credenza, which was along the back wall, and carefully popped a tile from the drop ceiling. Using the wall for support, she pulled herself up into the ceiling and replaced the tile.

She slowly crawled alongside the wall; the ceiling itself didn't have much support. She stopped at the near wall of the office Ski and Paul were using and pressed her ear down to the ceiling while balancing her weight against the wall.

"The staff opinions of the Bertrams seem pretty split." It was Paul speaking. "It doesn't seem as if anybody actually hates either of them beyond the normal office stuff that goes on."

"Yeah, that's about what I got too," Ski said. "But nobody's going to come right out and say they wanted to see him dead, either."

"But if they had, somebody else would've heard it, and I haven't caught wind of any interesting rumors beyond the fact that people are already talking about how the new kid went off to soothe Sara."

Shit, Brett thought. People were already talking. Just what she needed. And if anyone found out about what Ski had walked in on, the rumors would start flying, further implicating her.

Ski said, "Perkins, the personnel director, said she had thought about it but doesn't know how to cope with it all herself, let alone help anybody else. You ask me, though, she's just scared about keeping her job."

"I just can't believe nobody was in here the entire weekend. I'd think an ad agency would have people in and out at all hours of the day or night, even weekends."

"And you know the autopsy's gonna be a joke — what with the air conditioning turned up high. We won't be able to pinpoint an exact time of death."

The a/c was on? Smart move. Brett was a bit surprised building management didn't control such things, but it did make sense to have heating controls in an office where people were probably likely to work some very strange hours. And, since BB&B was the largest tenant, they probably could exercise a bit of influence on the landlord.

"Sara was the last one who saw him, when he left home at eight o'clock on Saturday for a meeting. Seems a rather strange time for me, especially in a place where no one works weekends." Paul seemed stuck on this weekend thing, probably because he didn't get them off too much himself. "What I can't figure out is why was Chuck killed at one place and taken to another?"

"Or so Peterson claims." Ski's voice sounded different now that she wasn't in the same room as Brett. More confident and cold. "Maybe she just wants to throw us off the trail — maybe she killed him here, then went to the Capitol and reported it. With such a vague time of death as would be established, it would give her an alibi — and what better alibi than the police themselves?"

"I can't believe she'd want to show herself as involved in any way."

"And that's the point. To make it seem so strange that we wouldn't believe anybody would do that. It would be an audacious move, but she seems the sort to try something that bold and daring, like it's an even bigger thrill to be so blatant and still not get caught."

"Next thing you'll be suggesting that he didn't die of a gunshot wound," Paul chuckled.

"No, it's pretty obvious that he did get shot, but I still want to see the autopsy report just to be sure. We should have it tomorrow or the day after."

That made sense, Brett thought. Lansing wouldn't have as many murders as Detroit, so their coroner wouldn't be so backed up and could get it done fairly quickly. But more intensive things would probably take a bit longer.

Sometimes it was interesting to note how many bizarre things one picked up if you ever had the need to know them.

Just then the door opened. Brett carefully maneuvered onto her back. It was quickly getting hot and uncomfortable up in the ceiling.

"Hey, Ski, I got the file you asked for," a new male voice said.

"Thanks, Dave."

"Alex said to just ask if you need anything else." The door closed.

"Peterson's personnel file?" Paul asked.

"Something's up with her, and I want to know what. I know that I know her from somewhere, aside from last night."

"Says here she's from Detroit."

"I knew it!" Ski proclaimed in triumph. Brett frowned and adjusted her balance on the edge of the wall. She was hoping to keep that bit of information a secret for just a while longer. She pulled out a tissue and wiped her brow.

"Looks like she just moved here a coupla months ago . . ."

"What're you looking at, her résumé?"

"Yeah. She went to Michigan State, worked at a coupla ad agencies and then moved out here. I wonder why?"

"That's what I'd like to know." Ski's voice sounded hard, cold.

"If she and Sara are lovers, and murdered Chuck, wouldn't it be stupid for Sam to come to work here right after?"

"She's hiding something, damnit, and I want to know what it is."

Brett sighed. Why were they so concerned about her? Why couldn't they talk about anyone else involved? Like, maybe, a little more on the relationship between Chuck and Sara? At least they could wait for the autopsy results. Of course, she already knew how, when and where Chuck died . . . Brett knew Allie would tell her cops often followed their instincts, but this was pushing it.

Well, she'd come here to find out what they knew, and where they were going. And now she knew. She carefully sat up in the confined space to start her journey back to Sara's office.

"Should we run a background on her?" Paul was asking Ski.

"Naw, I'll handle it. I'll call Detroit, 'cause I'm sure I know her . . ."

"If they've got the time of day down there for us."

"Don't worry, I've got my ways."

Shit, Brett thought. They were gonna go all the way on this one. She scrunched herself up and worked her way over to Sara's office. She could hear the fellow in the office in between talking on the phone, but she just wanted to get back down and go home. She started to pull up the ceiling tile then stopped.

"Honey, don't worry, everything will be all right," Sara said into the phone as she paced the office. "My hands are clean. They can't prove a thing because I didn't do anything." She paused, listening to the person on the other end of the line. "Now, just stay calm and don't worry . . ."

Shit. Brett carefully put the ceiling tile back and balanced against the wall, wondering if what she was hearing was what it sounded like — that Sara really did have a lover on the side. If the cops found this out . . . It might actually take some of the heat off Brett.

"No, you can't come over tonight . . . Honey, my husband was murdered. The last thing I need is for the police to find out about you. They're already suspicious enough as it is . . . Look, I gotta go now."

There was silence in Sara's office, but Brett could hear Sara's neighbor still talking on the phone. She was sure Paul and Ski were still in their room, and anyway, the last thing she needed was to be caught sneaking by them. No matter which way she went, she had a long crawl ahead of her in the hot, cramped, dusty —

She sneezed. As she reached to cover her mouth, to keep it quiet, she lost her balance and went toppling . . .

Right into Sara Bertram's office.

When she stood up from where she had landed on the floor, after hitting the desk, she saw Sara sitting across the room from her, staring.

"Sam. How nice of you to drop in so unexpectedly."

Brett ran her hands back through her hair and dusted off her jacket. "There's a perfectly logical explanation for this . . ." And she wished she knew what it was.

"Do tell," Sara replied, standing and coming toward her, a slight grin dancing across her face. It was obvious she had been crying again.

"Well, you see, I was trying to figure out where my computer printed to, so I followed the connection up into the ceiling . . ."

"And crawled all the long way over here following that little cord."

"Yes."

"But I believe your printer is right by your office."

Brett put a stunned look on her face and looked up toward the ceiling. She jumped back onto the credenza and started to lift the ceiling tile. "But look!"

"Get down from there, you moron," Sara said. Brett looked down at her. "You're lucky I like you, or else I'd can your ass in a heartbeat."

Brett jumped off the credenza. "So what are you going to do?"

"Ask what you were really doing up there."

Brett shrugged and sat down on the couch. "Saturday night I was taking a walk with my roommate and a guy ran by and got shot. He was dead by the time we got to him. So we followed the gunman, but he got in a car and raced off. We called the cops, but by the time we got back to the body, it was gone."

"And that body?"

"Was Chuck, yes. Ski was the detective on the scene, so she recognized me. That was what the little scene in here was about."

"So you figure they suspect you all the more because of what she walked in on earlier."

Brett nodded. "And when I noticed that they were

working out of the office near yours, and that you had left early, I figured I'd do a little eavesdropping to find out what they were thinking."

"People who have nothing to hide don't do things like that," Sara said, locking the door. She stopped just in front of Brett.

"I know."

"So what did you learn?"

"Not much. They are very curious about me and thinking we may be lovers . . ." She nearly choked on the word, wondering how Sara would take it.

Sara didn't blink. "And then you came over here and listened to my conversation."

"The end of it — something about your thinking the cops may suspect you." Brett began to fidget. Would Sara think of what else Brett had probably overheard? And why had she locked the door?

"Great. They suspect you, they suspect me, now they suspect you and me. I suppose if I canned you they'd make it into a lovers' quarrel."

"Or else say that now the deed was done, you didn't need me anymore." Brett stood and looked into Sara's eyes. Something about them comforted Brett. What was it about those eyes?

"There's something about you, Sam Peterson," Sara said as she reached forward and ran her fingertips under Brett's jacket and down her suspenders. "And now that I seem to be stuck with you, maybe we could give them something to talk about."

"I don't think that would be a wise idea," Brett said, pulling Sara's hands away.

"Ah, you're probably all show and no action anyway," Sara replied, turning from Brett and going to her desk. "You got the look down, but your carry-through needs work."

Brett slowly assessed Sara, with her long legs and trim body, then forced herself to think of Allie. No, she couldn't. "I'm not usually one to turn down such a dare," she told Sara. "But I fear I must let wisdom prevail this once." She turned and left the office.

"I don't want to talk about it," Brett said, holding up a hand to show she was serious. She took off her blazer and tie and threw them onto the couch then headed to the basement. Allie figured she'd had a bad first day at the office. Of course, with Brett, who had always been a night owl, any day that started with getting up in the morning was a bad day.

"Madeline doesn't think we're through with the corpse yet," Allie yelled downstairs after her. Madeline, their next-door neighbor and one of the first friends Brett and Allie made when they moved to Alma, was sitting in the kitchen sipping a cup of tea while Allie prepared supper. Allie was still intrigued by the missing body of two nights before, so she had invited Madeline over to discuss it. Madeline Jameson was an English/Women's Studies professor at Alma College with an active imagination and curiosity, as well as an amazing sense of perception and a touch of psychic powers.

"There is no such thing as coincidence," Madeline said, staring into the depths of her cup.

"Dinner's in ten minutes, Brett," Allie said. When she received no response she walked to the top of the stairs. "Brett?" Madeline followed Allie into the basement that housed Brett's workout equipment, where Brett had stripped down to her sports bra and athletic briefs and was currently doing bench presses. She wore black terrycloth head and wrist bands and leather weight-lifter's gloves. Allie picked up Brett's discarded clothing, carefully folding it. "Bad day at work?"

Brett lay back down on the bench and began lifting again. "I need to work out. Then I need a drink and a backrub, 'cause I'm gonna be sore as shit tomorrow," she said between reps.

"Then don't lift so much." Sometimes the woman was so damned stubborn.

"Not from the lifting, from falling off the ceiling."

Allie turned to look at Madeline, in case there was something she'd missed, but Madeline was staring at Brett.

"Boxer shorts?" Madeline asked.

"Not boxer shorts — athletic briefs. No fly," Brett explained as she rolled over and began doing leg curls.

Madeline looked at Allie, who shrugged. "She says they're comfortable and don't give her wedgies. All I know is she looks really hot in them."

"She does have nice legs," Madeline replied frankly.

"And I didn't even know you cared," Brett said, suddenly looking at Madeline.

"Then tell us what's going on," Allie said.

Brett began stretching. "I can tell you we ain't done with the body yet — 'cause I found it today."

"What?" Allie and Madeline chorused.

"He was the owner of BB&B. And guess who one of the detectives is?" At Allie and Madeline's continued prodding, Brett filled them in on her day while she finished her workout, thus making Allie forget all about dinner so it burned and they had to order out for pizza.

"Doesn't something like this always happen when you cook?" Brett asked as she cracked open a beer.

"Hey, I haven't burned the Hamburger Helper in eons," Allie said, placing the plates in the living room.

"There is no such thing as coincidence," Madeline repeated as she stared out the front window, her red hair giving her a wild look.

"What?" Allie asked. Madeline had a way of saying the most cryptic things as if they should make sense to everybody.

"Three events — the men at the ski lodge, the killing, and Brett's getting hired in at Chuck's company."

"Are you saying I've been set up?" Brett asked.

"Perhaps not knowingly, or by any particular person, but everything happens for a reason and there is a reason for everything."

"Great! There she goes again!" Brett cried, sitting on the couch and letting her disdain for Madeline's supposed psychic powers and knowledge be plainly known.

"It is just too coincidental for all these things to suddenly happen," Allie argued. "And you have to admit that Chuck's murder does seem too put-together . . ." It just had to be a professional job. Allie had immediately understood Brett's fear and frustration at Ski's interest in her. She was having a hard enough time accepting a quiet life for things like this to happen. If the cops looked into her past and identity too deeply they might come up with something that would make all her work on hiding herself come to naught.

"Yeah, yeah," Brett replied, bringing Allie back from her thoughts. "Most civilians wouldn't have it enough together to be able to kill him and get the body moved that quickly."

"But if it was a professional job, why have the body found at all?" Allie countered.

"Maybe as a warning?" Madeline suggested. Allie and Brett turned to her in surprise. "Well . . . I mean . . . Often dead things are left, or sent, as warnings . . ."

"She's got a point," Allie said to Brett. Allie was suddenly reminded that they had to be careful of what they said around Madeline, who already knew far too much about their pasts, which they were trying to keep secret from their inquisitive neighbor.

"Okay. Let's take this step by step," Brett said, grabbing another piece of pizza. "Forget about Tony for now. Someone wanted Chuck dead — so we need motive . . ."

"We don't necessarily need opportunity since they may have hired a professional," Allie added.

"Love or money," Madeline said. "The two classic motives."

"And revenge," Brett added, looking at the ceiling and sighing as she obviously remembered someone so out of control she killed for all those things. "Love, money and revenge. The true ménage à trois."

Allie suddenly found herself pacing. She was

worried. “Could they have set it up so you would first see the murder and then start at BB&B the next day?”

“It is possible, but highly unlikely and dangerous. To let Chuck run free like that, when we could’ve been anywhere, or he could’ve gone down some other street . . . He might’ve gotten away. There’d be other, more practical ways, to set me up.”

“What about his last words?” Madeline asked. “Didn’t you say they were something like ‘It’s just a phase’?”

“Yes,” Allie replied. “I don’t know. Maybe he was a little confused or something.” It just seemed that the words made no sense at all, which meant that their meaning was probably hidden and they’d have to dig to find it.

“I do not think we should forget about Tony,” Madeline said. “Especially if we are assuming that nothing is coincidental. Perhaps this Tony was hired to kill Chuck. Perhaps that is the transaction you witnessed earlier in the day.”

“Oh, come on, Madeline,” Brett said. “Figure the odds on that. I mean, what’re the chances we’d keep popping up throughout all of this? And then again a guy like Tony doesn’t come to town just to off the head of an ad agency. It isn’t his style.”

“Unless Chuck did something to really piss off somebody really big,” Allie said, her mind in a whirl. “Or he could’ve just been in somebody’s way.”

“You have mentioned that it appears to have been a professional job,” Madeline said.

“And Tony’s a professional.” Allie tried to remember everything Brett had said about Tony. It didn’t really seem like his bag to do a small, single killing like this one, but it probably wouldn't really matter if the pay was good enough. It had probably seemed like easy money.

It was after midnight by the time Madeline left and Allie and Brett retired to bed. As they lay in bed, they continued to talk, replaying all conceivable scenarios, with Brett filling Allie in on more and more of the day's events and Allie's questions jogging Brett's memory about specifics of the day.

They had considered Sara, and her mystery lover, who was the only suspect Brett had so far, since she didn't know enough people at the office yet to have any there. Sara said she didn't do it, but they could hardly take her word for it. Brett really didn't see any motives with the people at the office, unless, of course, it was something personal, but a crime of passion — such as it would be if he slept with someone's wife, or did something else really bad — wouldn't be so professional and laid out. People didn't usually hire hit men for things like that.

Perhaps Chuck had a lover on the side as well. Or perhaps he had some business on the side. After all, hadn't Alexandra begun to insinuate something about the state of affairs at the agency? Perhaps he hired Tony to blow up the mob's headquarters because he owed the mob money, and they found out about it and took care of him? Allie and Brett both chuckled over that thought — no one could be that stupid.

All they decided was that Brett definitely had to keep going to work until this affair was resolved. Otherwise, she'd be on top of the list of suspects. The last thing they needed was Brett's being booked, and fingerprinted. And who knew what else Ski and Paul could come up with if they examined too closely the fragile façade of Samantha Peterson's identity?

But all of this also seemed to indicate that perhaps they should start their own investigation. After all, what better way to clear Brett than to hand over the true criminal, complete with motive, opportunity and evidence?

That of course brought up the entire subject of how to get information and figure this mess out. Allie really didn't want them to get involved with breaking and entering, but Brett pushed the point, explaining that would be the only way they could have unlimited access to agency records and Chuck's office, in case it had been a business matter that got Chuck busted.

Allie countered that Brett could try talking with people at the agency to see if anything turned up that way. They could also utilize the Web to check out Chuck and Sara, as well as BB&B. Via the internet they could check out mainstream newspapers and magazines, as well as trade journals and business publications in general. Plus they could try to find out anything about Tony, although that seemed doubtful at best.

Allie also offered to check with some of her old police friends to see if anyone who seemed to be directly involved with the case had a criminal record. She suddenly realized she was almost happy to be lying in bed with Brett discussing all this. Although Brett's business degree gave her enough of a background to put to use in areas other than her prior profession, Allie's criminal justice major seemed ill-suited to anything but being a cop. Well, okay, maybe she could work for the courts, or a law firm, but that really didn't interest her.

During all the trials and tribulations of moving and getting things put away and situations dealt with in their move to Alma, Allie had been sufficiently occupied to keep her mind off the future — but now she had a chance to dwell on it and it scared her.

Chapter Five

Tuesday morning Brett started off the day by getting a list of all the agency's clients from Dick Pettibone, then she spoke with the other media people to find out what they had going on where. All very natural and easily explainable actions for someone in her position, even if it was somewhat unusual . . .

She already had information on most of the clients, as well as some news clippings about the agency, from the folder they assembled for prospective employees. But things often change, and changes are what sometimes causes the friction that gets people killed.

Alexandra Perkins flitted into Brett's office just before ten to give her the standard paperwork all new employees got and had to fill out, including a W-2, I-9, employee handbook and insurance paperwork, although she wouldn't be eligible for benefits for the first thirty days. She wouldn't get into the 401(k) program until her one-year anniversary. The very thought of such a thing made Brett feel very adult . . . and conservative. She hoped all this wouldn't make her start voting Republican.

A half-hour later, just as she finished perusing the employee handbook and was about to return the sheaf of papers to Alexandra, Dick came in and sat down in one of the visitor's chairs across from Brett, his large hands behind his head, his body stretched out in front of him.

"I just got a call and we've got a chance to pitch a local chain of convenience stores next week, so we've got to put together a plan. Think you can handle it?"

"Yeah, no problem." Brett hoped she sounded more sure than she felt.

"It's not a huge piece of business, but I like us to maintain a strong local presence. It helps for when the larger clients are in town, makes it easier to get tickets to events." Brett's confusion must have shown, because he continued, "You know, you spend some money with the local TV and radio stations and they throw tickets for concerts and such at you when you need them. We've already got a local dealership, but I would like to sweeten the pot a bit, make us even more important around here."

"Oh, of course. It's always a smart move to show clients a good time when they come to town, and it's even better still when it doesn't cost us anything. Which convenience stores are we pitching?"

"Quality Dairy. Nice family-owned company." Brett nodded, familiar with the chain. "I think, creatively speaking, it'd be a good idea for us to push the fact that they make their own baked goods, dairy and ice cream."

Quality Dairy was quite well known for one of its flavors of ice cream, Death by Chocolate, although Brett was fonder of their French Silk or Mackinac Island Fudge. They did things right, like not getting skimpy on the chocolate and fudge chunks.

"I seem to recall that you've worked on several grocery accounts, but I don't want you jumping to any conclusions," Dick continued.

"Oh, like just assuming the demographic target," Brett bluffed.

Dick nodded and stood, obviously getting into this. "Last time I was in one of those stores there were lots of men and kids. Especially with Michigan State in East Lansing, their target would be a bit different. Don't just go thinking the demo's women twenty-five/fifty-four. Look into it. We may need to run in the *State News* as well as the *Lansing State Journal*," he said, referring to both the college and local papers.

"Okay, I'll look into it first before I start."

"We've got a lot of research tools here. I think there's some hooked into the computer. If you have any questions, ask Toni. She's pretty good with that stuff." Toni was one of the media assistants. Dick left, leaving Brett to wonder how much of this Toni could do — as a learning exercise, of course.

* * * * *

"Hey, Toni, are you busy?" Brett said, walking up to the redhead's cubicle.

"I've got a bit of time, what's up?" Her desk was covered with papers. She was probably way too busy. Toni apparently noticed Brett's concern. "Oh, that's just some billing stuff. I need to get it out, but the accounting department's usually backed up, so I've got a bit of time on it."

"Dick just stopped by and asked me to put together a plan for Quality Dairy. He really wants me to investigate the target. Y'know, not make any assumptions that it's just another grocery demo of women twenty-five/fifty-four." Brett grinned as she said this. She knew she'd pick up the lingo quickly enough.

"Oh, yeah, QD. We've got a bunch of Scarborough books in the research library, but I've got all the media computers hooked into the data with Media Professional." To this Brett nodded sagely, as if she knew what was being said. "I mean, MRI would have info on convenience stores, I'm sure, but since we can get market-specific with Scarborough, it seems like that's what we should do."

Noting her use of "we," Brett realized Toni was trying to impress her. "Oh, yes, definitely. I think, though, that we should pull up the MRI info as well, though, since it'd be nice to point out how different this market is. Y'know, give the client a little show of how much we know and how well we know them. That sort of thing always makes them feel special." Brett glanced down at Toni's computer and noticed the many different icons, most of which she had only ever seen before on the computer she had just been assigned. “Tell you what, since I’m not really sure what all we’ve got access to here, do you think you could do me a favor and pull up some research so I can look it over.”

Toni’s eyes brightened, probably both from the term “favor” and from being given a challenge. “Oh, sure, no problem. I’ll get right on it.”

“But I think we should be careful, because they’ve might have more than one demo, and it might be nice to acknowledge this — y’know, put together something for their campus stores as well. After all, the students do run East Lansing during the school year.”

Brett spent the next hour with Toni, deciding which questions to pose to the computer while she posed as learning the software. Many things, though, started coming back to her from her old college days, especially with Toni’s friendly, aim-to-please attitude. The girl obviously wanted a promotion. She also apparently liked the interest Brett took in her career development, and the fact that Brett was giving her puzzles to solve.

As a partial repayment for her help, Brett took her out to lunch.

“You really don’t need to,” Toni said. “I really like playing with the computers and digging up facts.” At a larger agency, one with a research department, Toni would be ideally suited to research. But she said she liked the continual variety she experienced at BB&B.

“I just hope Sara can handle it all. I mean, I really feel for her, losing her husband and all, especially like that . . . and I liked Chuck too. I walked into work this morning and expected to see him. It was part of his routine to walk around and greet people in the morning."

"You're worried about your job, eh?"

"Yes," Toni said, looking down at her Caesar salad. "I hate to admit it, but I am. I mean, Sara's great and all, but it seemed like Chuck was more of the people person, the one who knew what to say to clients."

"I've noticed people tended to prefer one over the other."

"Oh yes." Toni grimaced. "I mean, Sara's great with the business end of things, but you can be a business genius and not be able to make a go of it because you don't know what people want to hear. And in this business, there's an awful lot of that going on." She smiled. "Before every presentation, Dick always looks around at whoever's going and says, 'Are we ready for this dog-and-pony show?' "

"What do you know about Dick? I mean, he seems like a really gruff sort, but . . ." Brett intentionally trailed off, wondering about people with motives at the agency.

"Well, I know he used to work for some big players down in Detroit, and I mean he worked on some big accounts. You know, big national clients that spend millions and millions annually . . ." She began playing with her salad, moving things around inside the bowl.

"Oh, c'mon, you can tell me. After all, we did just share this huge bonding experience of discovering how many people do most of their grocery shopping at Seven-Eleven." Brett reached out and lightly touched Toni's hand. "Although I still want to know if their home remodeling is just merely walls of Big Gulp cups." They had gotten a little silly with some of their fact-finding mission, an endeavor that came up with some truly surprising results.

"Well, I don't like saying anything . . . But . . . I've only been at BB&B for about nine months . . ."

"Toni. Come on. You can tell me." Brett took another bite of her burger and followed it with a sip of soda. "I won't rat you out. You don't seem the sort to play into all those office politics, and neither am I. Probably why we're both in media. We're just curious sorts."

"I heard that he was padding expense accounts and such. It was a client that figured this out, and that's why he's in Lansing now instead of Detroit. Nobody else would touch him since the agency lost the account after that."

After lunch, under the guise of getting a fuller picture of the entire agency, Brett started chatting up the creative and production people. And if they happened to drop names of companies and people they worked with from the outside, all the better — after all, she was new to this area, and wanted a better picture of everything happening in advertising in Lansing.

She then went to the accounting department and explained that billing was slightly different from agency to agency and she knew the only way to discover her particular duties regarding this was from them. They applauded her, then showed her around their areas, explaining everything in minute detail — including all that they went through because so many people just didn't know what they went through.

From there she went to talking up some of the A.E.s. All in all it was quite easy, because everyone was more than willing to bitch and complain about the workload and the unreasonable deadlines.

After all that, she didn't have any other suspects — no one was pointing fingers, everyone was scared about their jobs and about the future under Sara's leadership, unless, of course, they were scared about the future of BB&B and were already putting out résumés.

Of course, there was Dick's questionable past. She wondered who else had stories such as that?

Brett walked past the receptionist's desk, waving a quick hello to the once again calm and poised woman answering multiple phone lines simultaneously. On her way to get another cup of coffee, she wondered how to use the information she had gleaned that morning about Quality Dairy.

"Say 'Two all-beef patties,' " Brett suddenly heard a male voice say as she rounded the corner toward her office. She reflexively turned to face Paul and didn't notice the camera until the flash blinded her.

"Bastard!" She lunged forward, grabbing for the camera. Paul obviously didn't expect such a reaction and dove out of the way, almost knocking down two copywriters in his haste. Brett, more accustomed to knife fights, quickly regained her balance and turned to chase Paul down the hall.

Sara stepped out of her office and directly into Brett's path just as Ski also entered the hallway, curious as to the sudden disruption.

"What the hell'd you do that for?" Brett asked Paul, trying to dodge around Sara to get the camera.

"What's the problem, Peterson?" Ski asked, "I didn't think you had anything to hide."

"I don't," Brett growled, looking around Sara's shoulder. "I just don't like photos . . ." She quickly searched for an excuse. "I have bad luck with photos — something really bad always happens right after someone takes one of me."

"So it's not that you think you lose a bit of your soul?" Ski teased, seemingly enjoying having the upper hand on Brett for a change. Brett glared at her but allowed Sara to pull her into her office with an apologetic look tossed nonchalantly over her shoulder at the two detectives.

"Who the hell are you, really?" Sara asked as she locked the door behind them.

"What? Do you think that under this cool exterior of Super Media Planner there lies a darker side?" Brett quipped, glancing around Sara's office.

"No, I mean that I'm not buying how thoroughly Dick and Alexandra called to check your past employment when they hired you. I know how easily somebody can fake those things. As do Laurel and Hardy next door."

"So what's your point?" Brett asked from the window.

"Well, let's see. I've got half my employees sending out résumés because they think we're going down, and a bunch of clients are threatening to jump ship because they all worked with Chuck and don't know me from a hole in the wall —"

"You've just got to learn how to deal with them. Make them feel important. People like that. Reassure them."

"But I'm not that good with people."

"Correct me if I'm wrong on this, but I've heard you're the one who really ran things around here. Chuck handled the clients and you handled the business, so you already know your stuff. Let the clients know that."

"Easy for you to say." Sara was nervously rearranging the books in the bookcase.

Brett turned her to face her, leaving her hands on Sara's arms for just a moment. "I know it's easier to deal with facts and figures, because you can't take it personally if it doesn't work out. People can be scary. They can dislike you just for your shade of lipstick, and I've never known an equation to do that."

"You say that like somebody who knows." Brett could smell Sara's perfume swirling around her head.

"I do. I have dealt with impossible-to-please clients before. I think I've dealt with some of everything in my life, in fact." She sat on Sara's desk. "Dealing with clients makes me think of that old line about the world being a stage and us all being actors on it. You give them what they want. If they want the reassurance of a male there, then you make sure Dick's always with you when you see them. He's got the look and knowledge to pull it off."

Sara sat on the couch, her head in her hands. "I

just can't believe all of this is happening. It's like some awful nightmare. The sort of thing you hear about and don't really understand." She looked up at Brett. "I thought about it and realized what you heard the other day. But you have to understand that I did love Chuck. Yes, he was a bit older than me, but he had a way about him, a smile that made you know everything would be all right. He was my best friend, and we worked well together. We each were what the other lacked." The tears were again streaming down her face.

Brett went and pulled her into her arms, gently stroking her back and hair. "I know. Sometimes it seems ludicrous that we're expected to have one person be everything we need them to be. That a single person can fill so much of our lives." Sara's body was soft in her arms, her hair silky against her cheek.

Sara pulled away slightly, trying to compose herself but not giving up the comfort of Brett's arms. "So my husband's dead, I'm afraid of losing the one thing I've put more into than anything else, and I've also got police running around making people even more nervous, as well as thinking I could've killed my husband, and then I've got you not only crawling around the ceiling, but also trying to beat up the cops. Not exactly the most reassuring of circumstances." She picked up a tissue and dried her face, leaning back against the sofa's leather arm, studying Brett's face.

"If we could control life, it wouldn't be the adventure it is." Oh, God, she was starting to sound like Madeline. She needed to get a grip.

"What I want to know is what you're so worried about."

"Me? Worried? Nah. I just want to keep my job. Mortgage and all, you know."

"And I've got a bridge for sale. People who aren't worried don't usually eavesdrop and attack cops."

Brett raised an eyebrow. "Are you making insinuations against my character?"

"Not at all. I've just always found it useful to know what I'm dealing with."

"If I'm worried, then you must be as well. You have to admit, innocent people don't usually worry so much either."

"Samantha," Sara began, then paused. "That name doesn't really fit you, you know." To Brett's lack of reaction she continued, "You know I'm having an affair. I know you heard that the other day. I loved Chuck, and we shared many dreams and ambitions, but sometimes things aren't as easy as you'd like them to be. Because Chuck was murdered, and because I'm to gain a lot from it, it only makes sense that the police would think of me as a suspect. I'm also worried because I don't know who did it, or why. It makes me nervous."

"I'd guess it was a professional job. Not only because a random killer wouldn't bother moving the body, but also because his office, and his office alone, was trashed, but nothing appeared to have been stolen. Whoever it was meant business — it was a high-caliber gun that did Chuck." And she herself owned an unlicensed .357. Of course, the cops would need solid evidence against her to get a warrant to search her house, which was the only way they'd find out about her guns. And right now they appeared to be going on little else besides Ski's gut instincts.

"A professional job?" Sara repeated. For some reason, this seemed to give her pause.

"Yeah, I'd guess it was a professional job."

Sara again paused, the finally said, "And you're saying you think whoever it was, was looking for something in particular?" Brett nodded her answer. "Great. I wonder if they found it?" Sara looked grim and scared. She knew that if they hadn't found whatever it was they were looking for, there was a good chance she might be in their way when they came back to look again. Brett knew how men like that worked.

Give a little, get a little. She wondered what else she could get Sara to share with her.

"I need a drink. What can I get you?" Sara said, going to the bar.

"Glenfiddich on the rocks."

Sara turned and looked at Brett, who stood at the window. "You know, you never did answer my question."

"Which one was that?'

"About who you really are."

"I am who I say I am — Samantha Peterson." She took the drink from Sara and raised the glass to her lips. "I don't see why you would even question that."

"I've already told you why. And I don't know how you plan on getting it by the cops when you can't even get it past lil' ole me."

"You don't trust me, but it appears that you not only wish to befriend me but also want my help."

"You are a cynic, aren't you?" Sara replied, pouring her own drink. "A cynic, an enigma, a woman without a past whose tenuous present is built on fiction." She turned to face Brett, who had taken a seat in one of the comfortable visitors' chairs by Sara's desk. "I'm helping you because the walking lobotomies next door think we're in this together. They think the only way you got into the agency is through me, because it's obvious you aren't who you say you are."

"So you're saying you're innocent?" Brett looked up into Sara's deep brown eyes and suddenly thought of her favorite teddy bear, Boo Boo Bearski. When she was growing up, she always protected Boo Boo. Her father and brothers could do what they wanted to her, but they couldn't touch Boo Boo. She'd find him and hold him in her arms and protect him. He made her feel strong; he made her feel as if someone needed her. Sara's eyes were the exact same color as Boo Boo's worn, deep brown velveteen fur. The thought filled Brett with warmth as she remembered that favorite, and in fact only, stuffed animal of her youth.

Brett was ten when her eldest brother decided Boo Boo would make fine kindling for a fire. She had kept the melted remains of his buttons and his eyes for a long time, only discarding them after she bought her first gun, soon after graduating from college and going to work for Rick DeSilva. It had seemed like a time when the things of childhood should be set aside.

Brett looked into Sara's eyes and felt warm and fuzzy all over.

"You already know I didn't do it," Sara said, bringing Brett back. "Otherwise you wouldn't keep talking with me, telling me things."

Suddenly many things about Sara made sense, like the way she kept locking the door when Brett was with her. "Why do I have the distinct feeling you'd keep me even if I didn't do a damned thing around this place?"

"Because it's the truth," Sara answered frankly. "And can you blame me? You have thus far proven yourself to be audacious, resourceful, quick-thinking, athletic and compassionate."

Sara was again quite near Brett. They were playing a cat-and-mouse chase all across the room. Brett only wished she knew if she were the hunter or the prey. "And you've figured all this out in what? Twenty-four hours?"

"You'd be surprised what you can learn when a woman falls from your ceiling."

Brett let this slide. "Tell me, are you Chuck's sole heir?"

Sara turned from Brett. "No. We owned the agency together. When we met, he was an A.E. and I was a media supervisor at a pretty large place. His uncle loaned us the money to make a go of it up here."

"Now you're the one not answering questions."

"He split everything between me and his daughter, Rosa. His illegitimate daughter. He abandoned her and her mother when he was sixteen. She just tracked him down, oh —" She paused to think. "About a year and a half ago."

"Is she the third B?"

"Yes, she is. Chuck originally argued that BB&B sounded better than B&B. And in fact, we were the ones who started the entire 'Baffled, Bewildered & Bemused' joke. It seemed like a good way to build camaraderie among the staff. It wasn't until recently that I learned he did it hoping to one day find Rosa."

"So she walked into your life . . ."

"And Chuck wrote her into his will — at half of his half of the company, as long as she changed her name to Bertram from her mother's Gonzales."

Brett smiled. "This sounds like a soap opera."

"Then we should probably stop talking so much," Sara said as she ruffled Brett's hair. The air was tight with the electricity between them. "We have a lot in common." She took a deep breath and pulled herself away from Brett.

"You think you know nothing about who I am, but I keep feeling like you're trying to seduce me . . ."

"When you look at me, you look right into me. There's a connection, our eyes meet, and there's a flame. It's not just us looking at each other, it's something more . . ."

As Brett heard this, she thought about souls meeting, about something inside touching, reaching out to another.

"We're so much alike it scares you," Sara said. Brett went back to the window, at the view that never changed. She felt Sara walk up behind her but not touch her.

"I feel as if you know too much about me," Brett said, breathing hard, her pulse racing in her throat.

"And it scares you," Sara finished, still not touching her.

Brett turned to face Sara. "If we're so much alike, then you're a truly evil woman."

Sara smiled, slowly and sensuously. "Have dinner with me."

Brett looked at her. She told herself that Sara had information only she could give. She reminded herself she needed to protect herself and Allie, the love of her life.

"Tomorrow night," Brett finally replied. She felt like a moth drawn to a flame.

Chapter Six

Allie reached forward and picked up the Styrofoam cup of coffee. She took a sip and felt it curdle down her throat. Ugh, cold coffee. The lights were still on in the house, and the red Jeep Grand Cherokee was still parked in front of the garage.

She would've thought, from her quick observations of Sara Bertram, that she would've insisted on living in a much more elegant domain. Brett assured her, however, that half of Sara's public persona was an act. Sara was actually a businesswoman who wanted the company to succeed. If that meant putting more money back into it, then so be it. As for the Jeep, well, she was a wild woman underneath it all. Plus, one of the agency's clients had something to do with Chrysler.

She wished this could be a proper stake-out, with somebody backing her up on the following, and able to bring her fresh coffee and doughnuts. Why was she suddenly experiencing a craving for doughnuts? She hadn't had one since she quit the police force. Bagels were much healthier and kinder to the waistline.

Brett had called her from work, asking her to pick up Sara's tail at BB&B. Sara had left work at about five-thirty and gone directly to a parish close to her home, apparently to work out some of the details of the funeral with the priest.

Allie knew from personal experience that the first and last thing you needed when somebody close died was to worry about notifying relatives and setting up the funeral. You wanted time to grieve, but some of what got you through it until you could really deal with it was having to handle all of life's little problems — like caskets, priests and grave sites.

Even now the words made Allie shiver. Although she had always known, being a later-in-life child, that her parents would probably not live to help her through a lot of what she'd have to go through, she'd expected them to be around to see her turn thirty.

Allie had loved her parents. Yes, they had had problems with her coming out, but they accepted it, and accepted Brett as her lover when she was seventeen. They had just wanted her to be happy. She knew a lot of people said that but didn't really mean it, but her folks had. They admitted to needing time, but then they met Brett and approved of her, and her wanting Allie to go to college as much as they did, although they disagreed on one key point — her folks wanted her to go to the University of Michigan whereas Brett, as a Michigan State alumna, was true to her school. The point was that these very different people could come to agreement on one major source of contention — the rivalry between the schools was intense, to say the least — in favor of Allie's doing what was truly best for her. They just wanted her to go to college, get a degree and do something important with her life.

Allie and Brett broke up, and her parents were with her through that and the death of her best friend. Of course, it didn't help that her best friend, Cybill, died while cheating on her girlfriend with Brett's other girlfriend, Storm. Brett said she had already broken up with Storm by the time of the murders and Allie really did believe her. That was all water under the bridge anyway, because she and Brett broke up.

Several years later, when Allie was a Southfield policewoman, her mother died. Her father followed shortly thereafter. Maybe a month later, Randi McMartin approached her about helping to pull a sting operation on Brett. Of course, this was only after she and Randi had been dating for a while. It turned out that Randi had discovered Allie in Brett's past and felt she could do something to help her prove Brett guilty of multitudinous crimes.

Allie had gone along with it mostly because she knew Brett couldn't have done everything Randi thought she had. She knew there was a cold, hard side to Brett, a part of her locked away so tight that she might never let anybody fully in. She had seen it herself when Brett was interviewed, on the street, by investigative reporters on TV. She had seen the life, the humor, the sparkle disappear from her eyes.

She wanted not only to prove Brett's innocence, but to bring back the light in her eyes. No matter how long she went without seeing Brett, Allie never stopped loving her. She knew it was a mathematical impossibility that she would meet the love of her life when she was seventeen, let alone spend the rest of her life with her, but she knew Brett was it.

Her biggest problems sometimes were the self-doubts and second-guessing Brett did to herself. Allie tried to keep her mind open, tried to understand Brett and realize what she was going through. She knew Brett loved her but that sometimes Brett looked twice at other women and wondered if Allie really was the one. She wasn't so naïve as to not know that. She also wasn't so naïve as to not realize that if taken another step, some of what she and Brett went through would qualify as emotional abuse. But she also knew that Brett would never physically abuse her or intentionally hurt her.

Part of her attraction to Brett, as well as part of the magic Brett held for other women, was her mystery. Yes, she was attractive, and her graying hair only made her more elegant and sophisticated. It added an aura of maturity and grandeur. Her height gave her authority and power, whereas her eyes, which changed almost all the way from brown to green depending on her mood, created the idea of readability and adaptation. Plus she worked out, giving her a nice, tight ass, arms you could imagine strongly comforting you when the world was going wrong, and shoulders broad enough to cry on. And she knew how to dress, and the mannerisms to appropriate to make her everything she wanted to be. She wanted women to want her, and gained much of her energy from it.

But she needed to know she didn't need to, or have to, go it alone. She needed to realize fully that they were partners in whatever happened. She needed to trust in Allie's love for her, and believe in her love for Allie. That was one thing Allie never questioned — after all, Brett had already shown that she would die for Allie.

Allie could still hear the roar of thunder in her ears, see the bright bursts of lightning, feel the recoil of her gun when she aimed and fired at the only woman she would ever love so totally.

It was the night the sting had gone down. Allie had just discovered that Kirsten was responsible for much of what Randi was trying to blame on Brett. Brett walked in and saved Allie's life, for Allie knew Kirsten was going to kill her, but then Randi pulled up with the lights on her car flashing, and Brett knew what was going on. Brett always knew Allie.

Brett flew up the escape on the theater to the roof. Allie chased her. Brett shot at her, knowing there really weren't a lot of alternatives to the night. Brett had quickly realized what was going on, weighed the options, and understood that Allie would not shoot till she was shot at.

Brett planned on dying that night.

Allie had heard women tell the stories — "Oh, she'd do anything for me," "I'm her everything." She had heard these stories, but . . .

Her parents had tried to instill an honesty within her, an honesty not only in reference to others, but within herself. Allie tried to never lie to herself. But she knew lots of people said lots of things, never really meaning any of them, or just convincing themselves that they actually meant them.

That night on the roof of the theater, Allie didn't really have time to think, but she knew Brett and knew how much time Brett spent at the firing range. She knew Brett's obsessions and her strive for excellence. She was always her toughest judge. If she could live up to her own expectations, she could easily live up to anybody else's.

She also knew Brett carried a .357 Magnum and how long it took to fire off a round. That night Brett didn't fire off rounds and reload; her shooting was sporadic. In the time between that night and Brett's funeral, Allie had wondered about it. She had wondered what Brett had been thinking, doing.

Even she had to finally realize that Brett fired only wanting Allie to return fire, to shoot back. Something had to happen that night, they needed closure. One of them had to die. Brett realized this; there was no way out.

Kirsten showed up on the roof that night. Kirsten died that night, shot to death by Allie.

Allie had only ever killed two people in her life, Kirsten Moore and Carl Swanson, a child-abusing, wife-beating minister who tried to kill her and Brett a few months earlier.

Kill or be killed.

She hadn't become a cop to kill people, but to save them. She hadn't been able to save Chuck the other night either. She hadn't been able to save Chuck, her parents, or Cybill. She hadn't killed them, but she hadn't helped them either.

You can't save the world, she told herself again

and again. Her parents had died of natural causes. People died, it was a part of life. The hard part was settling for trying to help those she could. What she couldn't do was change the past.

She had done what she had to do to survive, and now she was beginning to forgive herself for it. It was going to be a long road, though. After all, she had gone this long barely acknowledging the pain or guilt. True forgiveness, the thought, was still a long ways off.

Allie glanced at her watch, 7:05. She glanced up and saw that the streetlights were just coming on. Brett wouldn't be making her move for a while yet. Allie was too scared by her sudden realizations to allow anything else into her mind. She tried to concentrate on her job, her duty, her sworn mission.

She had wanted to go with Brett to break into BB&B, knowing that, if caught, her past could stand up to the scrutiny that Brett's may not be able to. But Brett was better at such things and pointed out that there were only two of them and she wanted Sara followed. She also wanted a chance to look thorough the records of BB&B without anybody there to keep her away from any interesting pieces of information.

But Allie was worried — she and Brett had set up a fine house of cards built on the assumption that no one would ever ask many questions. Thus far, only Madeline's curiosity was piqued and Allie had the distinct impression that if it came down to it Madeline really wouldn't care. Madeline seemed, at the most, intrigued and amused by the challenge of discovering any of Brett's and Allie's well-hidden past. Allie was sure that once Madeline discovered the truth . . . She breathed hard at the sudden knowledge that Madeline would, someday, find out the truth about Samantha Peterson, that she was running from the law, running from her past as Brett Higgins.

They had money — they could probably live a life without ever working again. They didn't really have to make a living, interact so totally with others. After all, that interaction was what caused the problems . . . But it wasn't just work — look at the Tony thing; that happened when they were just out having fun. They couldn't stop going out just because somebody sometime might recognize Brett, because then they wouldn't really be living.

She stared up at the silvery crest of moon, and looked down just in time to see brakelights flash. She quickly glanced. All the lights in the Bertrams' house were off. Shit. She was so busy worrying about the future that she forgot about the present.

She turned the ignition and hurried after the red Grand Cherokee in front of her, amazed when Sara pulled out to the freeways and headed south, toward Detroit. But sure enough, interchange after interchange, Sara infallibly followed the signs leading to Detroit. It was a long drive and Allie hated having to waste so much valuable time merely following the taillights in front of her. Sara weaved in and out of traffic, doing well over the speed limit, suddenly making Allie glad it was she, not Brett, following Sara. At this speed, she'd be extremely lucky if she made it to wherever she was going without getting pulled over.

Sara followed I-96 for over a half-hour, right along

to 696, making her way through the northern suburbs of Detroit, heading east until she came to I-75, which she took north until exit 69, Big Beaver Road.

After that it wasn't very long before Sara pulled down a sidestreet. She must be nearing her destination, Allie thought. When Sara pulled into the driveway of an unspectacular residence, she pulled into the driveway of a dark house just down the street. Allie knew exactly where she was — it was her old Sterling Heights neighborhood.

She hadn't been very happy when Brett first suggested tonight's division of labor. Besides the fact that it put Brett at a distinct risk, almost everybody knew that following somebody by yourself, without being spotted, was nearly impossible. There were always missed traffic lights, or quick turns, or asshole drivers that slipped in at exactly the wrong moment. Thus far, Allie had been lucky, and she knew it was luck; she wasn't so arrogant as to try to convince herself otherwise.

But Brett was right, they really had no other choice. The only possible helper they had was Madeline, and not only did Allie not want to share much information with Madeline, she also did not want to put Madeline at risk, even though the middle-age professor openly admitted she really didn't care about things like that: "When it's time to go, you go."

Allie watched as Sara's neat, trim figure, clad in tight jeans, a white T-shirt and a denim jacket, left the sport-utility vehicle and entered the house. Allie carefully opened the door to her own car and stepped out, shutting it quietly. She then slipped across the few lawns separating her from Sara, dodging underneath windows so as not to disturb the neighbors.

At the designated house, Allie went to hide behind the front bushes, quickly stealing a glance inside. She stopped when she saw Sara fall into the arms of an attractive Hispanic woman with long black hair. By the way the woman held Sara, Allie suddenly knew that she was her lover. Brett had said Sara had a lover on the side, but Allie was willing to bet that she had no idea it was a woman.

The blinds were almost fully shut throughout the house, but the little gaps allowed Allie to peer through them and follow the two women to the living room.

The other woman began to slowly undress Sara, pulling her to the floor right there. Allie watched as they tenderly made love. She knew it wasn't as much about sex as it was about comfort, but she felt like a voyeur. Leaving would be the right thing, but she couldn't pull her gaze from the naked entwined flesh, the creaminess of Sara's breasts contrasting against the darkness of the other woman's skin and hair.

About an hour and a half later, at nine-thirty, Sara was again on the move. It had appeared that the other woman wanted her to stay, and they had argued about it, but Sara finally got dressed and left.

Allie snapped a picture of the woman standing in the doorway, another of the house, and quickly darted back over the neighbors' lawns to her vehicle. She had already jotted down the address of the house.

Sara drove across town to a far ritzier neighborhood and into the well-lit drive of a house that was more an estate than something so plebeian as a house. Allie parked outside the huge iron and stone border of the grounds. Peering through the metal framework, she saw Sara enter the house. Nobody else was in sight.

She quickly jotted down the address, as well as the license plate numbers and models of the other two cars in sight before she stuffed the notepad into her jacket and grabbed hold of the fencing. She jumped up and grabbed the top of the horizontal supports, then pushed herself up using her feet against the concrete posts for propulsion. When she reached the top, she wedged her knees in between the metal spires and sat up, straddling one of the dangerously sharp spires.

She jumped to the ground on the other side and dodged up to the house, going from tree to tree, using the thick trunks for cover. She quickly ran around the parked cars, grabbing the VINs before she went up to the house.

In the room that was apparently a living room, decorated in pristine white with a homey fireplace that was blazing a friendly fire despite the mild temperatures outside, was a woman sat on an overstuffed sofa flipping through a magazine. She looked bored as she carelessly went through the magazine, occasionally stopping briefly to glance at an article or picture that caught her eye. There was no sign of Sara. Allie snapped a quick photo before she continued along the front edge of the house to another room with its light on.

In a warmer, more masculine room, colored in darker earth tones, she found Sara standing, a glass of wine in hand, talking with an older fellow who leaned against an expensive desk. His white hair was brushed over in an attempt to hide the fact that he was balding, and his stomach came over the top of his expensive pants in a gut that so many older men have.

His and Sara's conversation seemed congenial enough and Allie wondered who he was. Obviously, he was important and wealthy, and he carried himself like a man who knew it. When Sara turned toward the window, Allie could see that she was crying. The man went to her and hugged her in a fatherly fashion.

Suddenly, a car roared up to the house and a man came barreling out of it. It was only when he stood in the light outside, ringing the doorbell, that Allie got a good look at him. Tony Marzetti. Somehow everything was linked together; Madeline hadn't been wrong.

Tony pushed by the butler who opened the door and forced his way into the study with Sara and the older fellow. He was clearly angry, but seemed to hold himself back in Sara's presence. He pulled the other man into a guarded conversation and Sara looked out the window, right at Allie.

Her eyebrows raised in alarm and she turned to the men, who quickly headed out of the study. Allie jumped to her feet just as she heard the snarl of dogs coming from the back of the house and took off running at a dead heat toward the fence she had come over in the first place. She heard the front door open behind her, followed by the bellow of men yelling. A bullet struck a tree near her head as the men spotted her.

Shit, the fence, Allie thought. She threw herself up, grabbing the top bar and immediately threw her leg up so her foot landed between the spires. She pushed up and over even as the dogs bit at the empty space she had just occupied.

She instinctively turned to the light that suddenly covered her.

"You!" Tony yelled in recognition from several feet away. He had a flashlight in his hand.

Allie jumped into the car and floored it.

Chapter Seven

Brett glanced around and at her watch. Ten-thirty Tuesday night. The guard was at his station, alone. About a half-hour earlier, he had turned toward the little television and leaned back in his chair. She was certain he could bolt, wide awake, to full attention to convince anyone that he was actually awake, but she knew better. He was sound asleep.

She double-checked her picks, flashlight, gloves and camera and approached the front door, which she could easily access with a code key, but she hadn't been given one yet, due to all the turmoil at the agency, and hadn't requested one because she didn't want to raise any additional suspicions. Anyway, a code-key would beep in the guards' office and record in the system her presence.

Fortunately, she was familiar with this sort of security system. And due to the guard's presence, the security was at less than optimal levels. Using her favorite set of well-worn picks, she opened the auxiliary emergency door. A well-positioned plastic wallet calendar kept the door from announcing her entrance.

She glanced toward the guard, who moved his head slightly in sleep. He was smart — instead of sitting upright so his head would tip and wake him, he was sunk lower in the chair so his head was balanced against the back, thus ensuring a less disruptive snooze.

Trained professionals, she thought, wouldn't have had much problem getting the body in there. Without cameras, it was the perfect set-up.

She carefully made her way across the lobby to the stairwell. She had worn all black, complete with a ski mask, to help conceal her identity if indeed she was spotted, but all went as planned.

The nine-floor hike up the stairs left her somewhat breathless — she really had to cut down on the smoking — but she finally entered the offices of BB&B, again using her picks, where all was quiet and dark. Fortunately, it was an older building; the security really wasn't much.

She made her way stealthily through the office. Her leather-clad hands easily picked the lock to the accounting department, her first stop. With her flashlight and her memory, she easily found her way around. She opened filing cabinet after filing cabinet, not quite knowing what she was searching for but hoping she'd know it when she saw it.

Accounts payable, accounts receivable, ledger books, balance sheets . . . So much material to cover. She glanced at her watch, then turned to the copy machine which, luckily, was still on because someone had been lax in their duties. She didn't know what she'd do if she had had to wait for it to warm up. She began to copy everything that seemed remotely interesting, since she didn't have the time to read everything. That could wait until later. For now, she'd just make her own records.

Although she shuddered each time a drawer creaked or groaned, she went back into the filing cabinets. She found bank receipts and files for accounts payable and receivable and photocopied anything that could possibly give her a lead. Working as fast as she could, Brett kept her ears and eyes pealed for anything unusual.

Normally, under circumstances such as these, she would have been fully relaxed and confident — after all, she had never been caught on anything so mundane as a B&E. But tonight she had a strange feeling. She must just be out of practice, she told herself, nervous because it was her first time in the field after a long hiatus, that was all. She was sure of it. But she couldn't help but hear Madeline say, "Trust your feelings, trust your instincts. They are your warning. They are your survival." Granted, she had said it months ago about something quite mundane. Actually, thinking about it now, Brett remembered it was the hot-water heater.

She quickly made the copies and returned the files

to their original positions, then went down the hall to Chuck's office, where she pushed aside the yellow police tape. Whoever paid attention to this shit anyway? she wondered as she played her flashlight around Chuck's office. She didn't pay much attention to the cops themselves, let alone their tape. Items no burglar would've bothered with — books, industry trophies, knicknacks and magazines — were strewn about the office.

Brett not only knew how to take a place apart to search it, she also knew what it looked like when she was done. And this place had not been burgled, it had been searched. There still existed a tiny possibility she was wrong, that this wasn't a professional job, but she sincerely doubted it. But she was also sure that whoever did this might have missed something because they didn't have the time, what with planting the body and all.

She went to the desk, although she knew the police had already searched it and had probably confiscated anything they found to be of possible use. Her fingers glided over the desk calendar with all its doodles, then through the papers on the desk. She couldn't find a Rolodex or an address book; items like those were probably among the materials confiscated. Looking at the surface of the desk calendar, a three-foot-long by two-feet-wide thing that covered most of the writing area of the desk, she wondered if anything he had written upon it would've left an indent. But of course that would've been too easy.

She glanced again at the much smaller, three-hole-punched desktop calendar. A date was circled in red. On a hunch she quickly jotted it down on a piece of paper she grabbed from his drawer.

She shuffled through the desk drawers, past Chuck's supply of candy bars and a bottle of Grecian Formula, and through all the miscellaneous desk supplies, still looking for something she wasn't quite sure of. In the bottom right-hand drawer she found a couple of magazines and quickly recognized them as being ones in which BB&B had placed ads for clients. The cops no doubt figured that they served other purposes; the top book was a copy of *Playboy*.

There had to be something here, damnit. A photo on the bookshelf caught her eye. She shined her flashlight on a picture of Chuck with a young woman who looked a bit like him: Rosa, his daughter. Brett took a step closer to get a better look at it.

Her foot crunched on something. She glanced down and the light from her flashlight glinted off tiny pieces of glass surrounded by an expensive oak frame. She picked it up. The frame was rich carved oak, which weighed heavily in her hands. The photo showed two men at a golf outing: Chuck Bertram and a man whose image still gave her chills, Jack O'Rourke.

Brett took a deep breath as cold rage slowly dribbled down her spine. There was no love lost between her and Jack O'Rourke. In fact, once upon a time he set two of his boys out to do her in. She slowly chuckled as she remembered how she and Frankie had taken care of Johnny and — she searched her memory for his name. Leo. How could she not have remembered that ugly puss? The man she had seen with Tony Marzetti the other day at the ski lodge was Leo, who worked for Jack.

How could she forget a man who had once tried to kill her?

She tried to brush off some of the glass, and that

was when she noticed the bright pink fluorescent paper peeking through a rend in the photo. Most people didn't use a mat that color.

Carefully she removed the picture of Chuck and Jack from the frame and pulled out the folded sheet of paper. It was a flyer for a play, *Just A Phase*, with a picture of five people. Two older women, one black and one white, stood at either side, looking quite appalled, and in the back was a really bad flaming drag queen. In the foreground sat a rather cute couple, both female, both rather femme, albeit one was trying to look butch in a shirt and tie. Yeah, they were cute, although neither was quite Brett's type, maybe good for a one- or two-night stand, but . . .

In the dark, immovable silence she heard the beeping of the elevator stopping at the ninth floor. Its doors opened and someone entered BB&B. Each noise echoed down the carpeted hallways like drumbeats. Brett froze, trying to figure out what to do.

She stuffed the photo and, on second thought, the flyer into her pocket, then switched off the flashlight. Her heart was pounding. If it was just the security guard on his rounds, there should be no problem in simply hiding underneath the desk. He would only glimpse into the office for a few moments, then continue on. He'd never notice her presence.

But what if it was someone else? Her mind raced as she reminded herself of the risk of assumptions. She padded silently to the door and glanced down the hallway. There was no mistaking the athletic, brown-haired detective who was heading right for Chuck's office.

Brett was suddenly glad for Ski's cockiness — the detective hadn't turned on any lights. The only illumination came from the lobby, where the lights were never dimmed. Ski gazed about slightly, so Brett took a chance and slipped out of Chuck's office and hustled silently down the hall, away from Ski.

Because Chuck's office was in the corner, it only took Brett a second to get out of Ski's line of sight. Ski stopped at Chuck's office, looked in and flipped on the lights. She briefly fingered the ripped police tape and entered the office.

Brett carefully inched her way down the hallway till she could see Ski within the office. It seemed she was looking for something in particular. She bent down to examine the frame Brett had carelessly discarded, picked up some of the glass shards and let them slide through her fingers, a thoughtful expression on her face.

Brett stood in the hallway barely breathing. She couldn't go out the front doors of the agency; the beeping would announce her presence, and it would be too risky to try to disarm it. Even a few seconds' exposure could give her away. She silently beat it down the hallway. Had she been discovered?

Brett stole into the creative department and looked back toward Chuck's office. Ski was scanning the hallway, as if trying to decide whether or not she was alone, and if not, who was there and where they were. Brett focused her attention on her surroundings, noticing all the artistic supplies and photography props and other miscellaneous items. She glanced up at the ceiling. No, it would be too easy to get trapped up there, as she had already discovered.

A hank of strong rope lay coiled on the floor. It was more than a hank, in fact; it was a whole reel. She didn't even bother wondering what those weird creative types were up to with it; she merely lugged it up over her shoulder and went to the door.

Ski was on the move, turning on lights and peering into offices as she went. Remembering Sara's heavy oak desk, Brett waited until Ski was out of sight, then scuttled toward Sara's office. Just then she saw the light go on in the creative department. Ski was hot on her tail — she had to move fast. She gingerly locked the door to Sara's office and went to the desk.

She secured the end of the rope to a leg of the desk, trailed it to another and tied it off there as well. She went to the window, which was stuck closed. Swearing under her breath, she pounded the window open. Hearing a nearby office door kicked open, she tossed the rope out the window, took a deep breath, grabbed the rope and plunged. She hung for a moment, suspended in space nine stories off the ground, the rope dangling below her, when she heard the door to Sara's office kicked in. It wouldn't be long before Ski figured out where she had gone.

She was glad for her leather gloves. Because of them she was able to quickly rappel herself down the rope to the ground. It seemed like hours but she knew it was perhaps a minute before she was only a few feet from the ground, at which point she dropped and took off running to her car.

Her heart still racing even after an almost two-hour drive home to Alma, at twelve-thirty Allie pulled down the street she and Brett lived on. She saw Brett's taillights flash as she raced into the driveway.

Apparently Allie wasn't the only one who had a bad night.

"Quick, I think Ski's behind me!" Brett called as she ran into the house. The door was open and the lights were on already — Madeline was waiting for them in the living room. Brett and Allie rushed through the room into the bathroom.

"We've been home all night," Brett called as she yanked her clothing off and dumped it, her gun and the photo and flyer into the laundry bin in the bathroom. Allie did likewise and the two women jumped into the shower.

The hot water felt good on Allie's body, pushing away a lot of the tension of the night. Brett, seeming to know what she needed, pulled Allie into her arms, and their naked bodies melted together under the force of the spray.

"Ski almost caught me at BB&B," Brett said softly. "I think she raced me here to try to prove it was me."

"Your not being home, or anything else like that, isn't enough to prove it was you."

"I think she's grasping at straws, just pissed that I got away without her being able to get a positive ID."

They got out of the shower and donned matching white terrycloth bathrobes, then entered the living room. Joan Lemanski was talking with Madeline. Allie thought Brett did a marvelous job feigning surprise, pretending that she hadn't expected Ski.

"We seem to have an unexpected visitor, honey," Brett said as she leaned back against the wall and took Allie's hand in her own. "You do remember Ski from the other night, don't you?"

"Yes, I always remember people who call me a liar." Allie slowly assessed her as she assessed Brett.

Allie did not like the looks Ski was giving Brett, whose robe only went halfway down muscular thighs and revealed forearms that had not an ounce of fat on them. Who did the bitch think she was?

"I suppose you're gonna say you two have been home together all night long," Ski said.

"How can we help you?" Brett replied.

"I've already told her that we've been playing Trivial Pursuit since dinnertime," Madeline said.

"Do you always take showers when you have company?" Ski asked.

"Madeline's not company," Allie replied, taking a step forward. "She's family. And she's spending the night." She wanted Ski out of their home, with her drab clothes, bad attitude and all.

"You didn't mention that," Ski said to Madeline.

"You didn't ask."

"Now we would like to get to bed, detective," Allie said, guiding Ski to the door. "So unless you have a warrant to be here, to search the premises, I think you should go."

Ski slowly looked over Brett and Allie, as if she wanted to memorize every detail about the two women, before she turned and headed to the door without a single word. Allie wondered if Ski had a lover, or if she was even out to herself. Suddenly, she could almost feel sorry for her, knowing that they weren't really making her job any easier. Having once been a detective herself, she could relate to that.

As soon as Ski left, Brett turned to Madeline. "What are you doing here anyway?"

"I just had a feeling," Madeline replied with a smile.

Although Brett wanted to get the film from Allie's

camera developed ASAP, Madeline told them there wasn't a chance in hell they could get it done that night in this small town. Allie looked at the photo Brett had brought and identified Jack O'Rourke as one of the men she had seen earlier.

Allie filled Brett in on the link she had developed between events, saying they were not merely coincidences, even while Madeline insisted there was no such thing as a coincidence. Then Allie realized she couldn't fully inform Brett on these matters with Madeline around. But, eventually, Madeline allowed them a few moments to talk in private and they began to lay the plans for the next day.

Madeline didn't ask any questions about how they got the information she did, or where Brett and Allie learned the techniques they had employed that night, probably because she knew they wouldn't give her any answers.

Chapter Eight

Wednesday morning, Allie sat staring at her computer screen, which showed a picture of Jack O'Rourke at the recent trials of Detroit mafia types. Jack's role was minor in the huge saga, but Allie was trying to find out everything possible about Jack, Tony, Sara and Rosa.

After Madeline left the night before, Allie and Brett had sat down and thoroughly compared notes on the night. Allie described the people she had seen Sara with, as well as the houses she had gone to. Brett immediately identified Jack O'Rourke's house by its locale and general description, as well as Jack himself.

Brett had gotten a strange look on her face when Allie told her Sara's lover was a woman. It seemed as though she wasn't really surprised by it. But she was surprised by Allie's description of Sara's lover.

"That's Rosa, Chuck's daughter," Brett said.

"Oh, my God. Are you sure?" Allie asked.

"Well, there's a chance that it's not, but it sounds like the photo of her I found in Chuck's office. At least, I assumed it was Rosa."

Allie's purpose in digging up information was that she hoped she might find out some things that Brett didn't know. Nobody knew everything, and when the two of them compared notes later that evening, they'd be a lot further along.

"Hello?"

Allie just about jumped through the roof when she heard the voice come from the living room. "Madeline, you scared the life out of me!"

"I decided to cancel office hours today because it seemed to me that you could probably use an extra hand in going through everything from last night."

" 'Everything from last night' ? Madeline, what makes you think there's anything to go over from last night?"

"No matter how hard you and Brett try, you will eventually tell me all. Until then, I am forced to make certain assumptions. In this case, I am assuming you and Brett would neither be visited late at night by a police officer, nor ask me to lie to her, unless there was something you were trying to hide. Therefore, you gained some information that you are probably hard at work analyzing and, furthermore, chances are you could use a hand in this analysis."

Allie stared at Madeline in wonderment. The woman was just too much. "But why do you always assume we're hiding something?"

"Because you usually are."

Allie laid a cold stare on her neighbor. "It's just killing you that you're not involved, isn't it?"

"I would much rather it be killing *me* that I am not involved than for it to end up killing *you* that I am not involved," Madeline replied with a wry smile. "By the way, that was a very nice, if not quite effective, attempt at changing the subject."

Allie inspected the redhead. From what she already suspected of their involvement in this murder, this could very well end up being a dangerous escapade for them all. She and Brett were used to living life on the edge, to being in the line of fire, but Madeline was a college professor . . . Still, as Allie glanced at the piles of photocopied ledger sheets and thought about the film that still needed to be developed, and finishing the internet search, she realized she could use some help.

"Do you know anything about accounting?" she finally asked Madeline.

"Allie?" Madeline called a few hours later.

"Yeah?" Allie replied, barely looking up from the computer terminal. Jack had quite a history and was definitely in competition with Frankie on some of his enterprises, from pornography to drugs to illegal gambling. Well, okay, Frankie seemed to have cut down on much of the operations, but Jack would've been in competition with Brett and Rick DeSilva.

"Is it possible that Brett might've missed a few clients and vendors?" Madeline was still going through the copies Brett had made in the accounting department and comparing those to Brett's previous lists of the clients and vendors of BB&B.

Allie shrugged. "Yeah, I'm sure she might've."

"Perhaps twenty of them?" Madeline asked, entering the room. "A lot of money comes and goes through those people and, quite frankly, I really do not see how some of them could be such big clients."

Allie went with Madeline to the living room, where Madeline had spread papers across all available surfaces. Madeline began walking Allie through what she could tell of things at BB&B, like apparently only Sara and Chuck could sign checks to pay vendors. Because of the way the papers had come, the way that Brett had photocopied them, it appeared that different people handled different ends of the accounting spectrum — that one person handled accounts payable whereas another handled accounts receivable. Although to the best of Allie's knowledge, this made sense and was standard operating procedure, she quickly realized that it also meant that the right hand would not necessarily know what the left hand was doing.

The papers were neatly organized, each paid invoice accompanied by a photocopy of the check that paid it. Allie could imagine the women in the accounting department, very neat and tidy, doing everything according to procedure like some great machine.

Allie was surprised to discover that, in addition to regular BB&B Advertising business, Chuck had also had a thriving business as a media consultant. She remembered Brett saying that it was Sara who had the media background; Chuck had been an A.E. This did not make sense.

She went back to the master ledger sheets. A great deal of money came in through Chuck's consulting, as well as from a few other clients Brett had not mentioned. And among the paid invoices were quite a few vendors Brett hadn't mentioned either.

But it was when Allie looked at the bank statements that red lights started going off for her. There weren't a lot of them, but still enough cash deposits of a large enough total sum to make her wonder. Beyond that, by looking at the checkbook, Allie was willing to bet that Chuck and Sara drew their pay in cash as well.

People in advertising wouldn't do business in cash. Yet cash came in, and Allie suddenly realized that it went out to fictitious vendors and other miscellaneous expenses, like business lunches that cost far too much. She again went over the vendor listings. Paradise Theater, Detroit, Michigan. She couldn't believe she had missed it before.

She didn't want to bother Brett at work, but she had another idea. "Madeline, I need to make a couple of phone calls. Do you think you could run out and get us sandwiches? I'm famished."

Madeline gave her a look that made it perfectly clear that she knew what Allie was up to, but she didn't fight too hard to stay, which almost surprised Allie. As soon as she was gone, Allie picked up the phone. She had read somewhere that an estimated

$110 billion was laundered each year in the U.S. She had never been able to understand it entirely, how people got away with it, but seeing this showed her one way of how it might be done, as well as proving to her that some people, including bankers and accountants, don't look too hard for it, so people got away with it.

She suddenly realized that Brett would have to know something about money laundering; after all, laundering was necessary to convert illegal income into legal income so you couldn't be caught for the crimes you committed in earning the money.

The phone rang three times before the deep, booming voice thundered over the line. "Dis is Frankie."

Allie grinned again, imagining the big fellow sitting at his desk, grimacing into the phone, putting on a full display of his business persona. "Heya, Frankie, this is Allie."

"Hey, Allie! How the hell are ya doin'?"

"I'm good, Frankie, but Brett and I have a problem . . ."

"Why the hell don't that surprise me?"

Allie grinned. She liked Frankie. "Frankie, you don't use an ad agency for anything, do you?"

"Are you nuts? You think I'm gonna trust some assholes to help me run my business? The only type a advertising I do, I tell them what I want it to look like, and they handle the rest. I like to go directly to the guys who put together the magazines . . ."

"Which magazines?"

"*Panorama, Cruise, Metra* — y'know, the sleazy

little things filled with ads for phone sex, bookstores and shit. Oh, shit, yeah, I guess they have somebody put together the ads for them."

"And you don't take checks?" Allie asked, jotting notes down on her pad.

Frankie let out a low chuckle. "Do I look like a fuckin' moron? Anyways, the shits that come to me like to pay cash, 'cause then their wives can't figger out what they're up to." He paused briefly, "Well, okay, yeah, I take Visa these days, but we don't do a lot of that."

There were so many aspects of Frankie's business that Allie had never before fully considered. "One more thing — do you know Jack O'Rourke?"

"Hell yes! Jack's a sonabitch that I'm gonna cream one of these days. Boy's getting too damned big for his pants and it's pissing me off. Don' get me wrong, I been playin' it cool since Brett retired. I know I'm not as big a businessman as Brett or Rick, but I still ain't one to be messed with, and Jack's tryin' to mess with me, moving in on my territory and shit." He let out a low, evil chuckle. "In fact, I remember one time when Jack sent Johnny and Leo after Brett. Well, first they took out one of our suppliers, then tried to do Brett, but she got away. So we figured out who they was and kicked the shit outta them. Put their asses in the hospital for quite a while. But not before they told us they worked for Jack."

"What's Leo look like?"

"Short, stocky, and man oh man is he ever ugly. And you know I don' say that about nobody."

Allie wasn't used to Frankie's ever being so talkative. "Frankie, is everything all right?"

"Yeah." He paused. "It's just that, well, I miss you

two. I wish you'd come back home. I don't see where Brett can be in that bad shape if anybody knows she's really alive. I mean, I been thinking about it and, well, anything that might've gotten her in trouble got burned up with the theater and all . . ."

"I miss you, too, Frankie."

Brett sat at her desk, tapping out an urgent beat with her Cross pen. She hated wasting time trapped behind a desk. She should be out on the streets, finding out things, putting this all together.

Especially now that she knew Jack O'Rourke was involved. She still had some unfinished business with him. Business from many years ago, when Jack told a couple of his associates to deal with Brett Higgins. She ran a hand along her thigh, knowing her fingers traced the line of a scar but unable to feel it. A friend of hers had butterfly-stitched the wound for her, but the nerves hadn't been quite right ever since.

She got up, closed her briefcase and headed to the door.

"Going someplace, Peterson?" Ski asked, blocking her path so that they ran into each other.

Brett pulled back and looked into Ski's eyes. "What's it to ya?" she said, trying to regain her composure.

"Well, I was hoping you could help me with a few questions I've got." Ski was obviously having great difficulty not looking away.

"Cut out the doughnut diet and you might be able to get a date, or else go back to men," Brett said, although she thought Ski's figure, what she could see of it under the oversized clothing the woman wore, was perfect. She just needed to say something to break the tension.

Ski stared directly at her. "We both know you were here last night and that you removed crucial evidence from a crime scene."

"Prove it or leave me the hell alone." Brett pushed past her and slammed right into Paul, who'd been standing just behind Ski.

"Well, maybe you'd like to let us know how somebody who's never worked in advertising before ends up in a nice cushy job like this," he said, deliberately stopping her.

"A nice cushy job? My ass. I'm sweating bullets over this big Quality Dairy plan they got me working on — not only do I have to do the plan itself, but also all the research, since this place doesn't have a research department."

Toni walked up and handed Brett a manila folder. "Here are the costs you asked for. I'm really excited by this because I know they're going to love it."

"Why?" Ski suddenly asked.

"Sam's come up with some alternative media ideas, such as tying into the football games on campus and using some different outdoor venues to get the message across."

"As you can see," Brett said, "we're quite busy. Toni and I need to sit down and pound out the rest of this presentation." She motioned for Toni to follow her into her office, then closed the door behind them.

* * * * *

Later that afternoon, Brett sat at her desk, flipping through the newspaper. She glanced at her watch, then the calendar. She felt trapped. She picked up the local section of the *Detroit News/Free Press*, the so-called scab paper because it had continued to publish regardless of striking workers, a situation that ended badly with hundreds of people injured and jailed. The employees were still unhappy, even though it had been going on for over a year.

Her phone rang. "Sam Peterson," she said, answering it.

"Brett, I think I've got something figured out." Allie's voice was soft and smooth, but she could tell that her lover was deep in thought about something.

"What's going on?"

"Money laundering. Madeline and I've been going over the books you copied last night, and I'd be willing to guess that's what Chuck was up to."

"Laundering for Jack," Brett said, thinking. That would explain his connection with Jack all right. But why would Jack be using a Lansing ad agency to do his laundering?

"What I'm wondering," Allie said, bringing her back, "is how much Sara's into it. After all, she did visit Jack last night."

"And what did Chuck do to piss off Jack so much? And why is Tony doin' small hits like this?"

"Yes, exactly. Anyway, I just wanted to let you know what I've found. We're still working on putting all of this together enough for the police to get warrants to search the books and records of BB&B. It's a pretty tricky paper trail."

"Okay, thanks. I think I'm gonna go have a chat with Sara."

"You're not going to tell her what we've found, are you?"

"I'm gonna play it by ear. Jack's a serious boy, and if she's got something he wants, she's really not safe."

"Brett, honey, I know you're not going to like this, but I need to say it anyway. I think you're just going to keep raising suspicions. You need to take a step back and let me handle this."

"I've got more inside info on all this sorta stuff, hon."

"But they're already suspicious of you, and your nosing around so much is making you even more obvious. You can't really afford to have the police getting too much into your past."

Brett grinned. "You were right. I don't like it. And I can't do it."

"You're such a butch."

"Uh huh."

When Brett went to Sara's office, the door was closed. She put up her hand to knock but heard voices emanating from within. The only snatches she could catch were to do with the fact that Chuck's body had finally been released and the funeral was set for tomorrow, Thursday, in the morning.

She knew she couldn't keep eavesdropping right at Sara's door, so she went to the kitchen to get a cup of coffee while she waited. She heard Sara's door open and she went to talk with her, but changed her mind as soon as she realized Sara's visitor was the good-looking, dark-skinned woman she had seen in the photo in Chuck's office. Chuck's illegitimate daughter, Rosa. Brett followed her.

Rosa was obviously perturbed about something as she rushed through the office to the elevators. In the parking lot, Rosa jumped into a red Mustang and floored it. Brett raced to keep up with her. Clearly distraught, she darted in and out of traffic, gunning her engine and running yellow lights.

Finally she drove down a side street into a slummy neighborhood and stopped in front of a lesbian bar, Club 505. Brett drove around the block, then parked nearby in a lot. She pulled out her Beretta from the glove compartment and attached it to her ankle. She then took off her blazer and tie, loosened her collar, ran her fingers back through her hair, bringing a few wisps of her bangs down on her forehead, and dabbed a bit of cologne along her neck and rolled up her sleeves. She crossed the lot and entered the bar.

Rosa, with her long, black hair providing a veil to her features, was sitting at a corner table, coldly regarding the empty bar while she drank a beer and smoked a cigarette. There were two empty shot glasses sitting on the table in front of her. Rosa looked up when Brett entered, and Brett met Rosa's blank stare and nodded, then sat down at the bar.

"Heya, what's up?" Brett asked the bartender, a friendly woman in a lavender T-shirt, jeans and a thick black belt. A whip key ring hung from a belt loop. Brett recognized her from her and Allie's infrequent visits here. Her name was . . . What was her name?

"Ahhh, it's goin', it's goin' . . . Whatcha drinkin'?"

"Molson Ice."

Debbie, that was it. Debbie grabbed a bottle from the cooler, popped the cap and handed it to Brett, who tossed a couple of bills on the counter.

"Thanks, Deb."

"Anytime, Sam," she replied. Brett did a quick double-take. She remembered her name — she must've made quite an impression on her previous visits. Deb gave her a quick smile and wink as she made her way over to Rosa's table.

"Mind if I sit here?" she asked Rosa, whose look clearly stated that yes, she did mind, but Brett sat down anyway. "You're off to an early start," she said, fingering the shot glasses.

"It's been a really bad week," Rosa finally replied, tossing back the rest of her beer. She got up to get another, but Brett quickly jumped to her feet and took the empty bottle.

"Allow me." She returned a few moments later with another for each of them, even though she had barely tasted her first one. What was bothering this woman so much that she was drinking this heavily at twelve? And why had she stormed out of the agency like that?

"*Gracias.*" She sat back in her chair and silently assessed Brett. "I bet you've never been dumped in your entire life."

Brett smiled. "It all depends on your perspective." She paused for only a moment, knowing she had to move this conversation to where she wanted it. "That what happened to you?" she asked, indicating the empty glasses.

"Yeah, I got dumped. After all I did for the bitch, I get dumped."

"Were you together long?" Brett asked, wondering why Sara had dumped Rosa.

"Well, we were never a real couple. I mean, she had a husband —"

"A husband?"

"Yeah, she was married . . ."

"But she's not anymore?"

"Let's just say the husband is out of the picture," Rosa said as she peeled the label off her beer. "We originally met through him, and maybe I first noticed her in order to get at him, but . . ." She trailed off, studying her beer. "He thought I wanted the best for him."

"So they're divorced?" Brett asked, prodding, trying to keep Rosa talking. She must know something. After all, Chuck must've loved her at the end, regretted what he had done. He had wanted her to have his name and wrote her into his will.

"Let's just say that they're now separated."

Brett signaled for Deb to bring a couple of shots and another beer for Rosa. The two women polished off the shots, and Rosa was starting to get cocky.

"You play?" she asked Brett, indicating the pool tables across the room.

"Yeah, I do," Brett replied, with her most sincere look. Rosa smiled at her as they walked over to the table and selected cues.

Rosa looked up at Brett after breaking. "The things we never know till it's too late. I figured she couldn't really love him that much if she was having an affair on him."

"Love can be a mighty strange thing." Brett neatly banked a shot into the far pocket and began lining up her next shot. Rosa was beginning to show the effects of the alcohol.

"I can't believe she's never figured out what he was doing. But I honestly don't think she has," Rosa continued. "I mean, the agency obviously doesn't have enough clients to be paying out such salaries. Where did she think he was getting the money from?"

"So where was it coming from?" Now they were onto the important stuff. Maybe she could get something more.

Rosa shrugged. "She just won't face facts," she said, finally getting another chance at the table. "I just think it's interesting that he told me, but not her." She missed her shot and stood holding the cue across her body, looking at Brett.

"Never any telling about people. I could just as easily ask you why you're telling me all this."

Rosa smiled. "Because you're a good listener and I need to talk. I need to admit to somebody that I talked him into doing something really stupid, that I thought that was what I wanted, but now I'm not so sure."

"What did you talk him into doing?" Brett said, pulling Rosa by the cue closer to her. She whispered, "Why do you need absolution?" Brett didn't move, allowing the tension to build between them. She pulled the cue from Rosa's hands and leaned into her so Rosa was forced to lean back against the pool table. "Tell me," Brett whispered again, letting her breath caress Rosa's neck.

"I talked him into withholding money from the mob," Rosa growled, pulling back just enough to look Brett in the eye. "And now she's fucking dumping me, saying she's not sure she can go on!"

"Yeah, right," Brett whispered, her hands finding Rosa's hips, pulling them closer. No one could be stupid enough to take money from gangsters.

"He was laundering money for them. I told him he was taking all the risks so he should get a larger chunk. He started siphoning their money — slowly, but I guess they figured it out." She was leaning against Brett now.

Brett wrapped her arms around Rosa in a hug. "How could anyone think they could get away with something like that?"

"He thought he was so damned smart, and that they wouldn't touch him anyway, 'cause he's Jack's nephew and all."

Holy fucking shit. There it was, the connection Brett had been looking for. She figured she had everything she was going to get from Rosa. She wanted to bolt, but Rosa was crying against her shoulder now.

"Let me call you a cab, honey," Brett murmured.

"He was my father," Rosa said, trying to pull herself away from Brett. "He was my father and he abandoned my mother when she was pregnant. He was a bastard but I still loved him."

Brett wrapped an arm around Rosa's waist, guiding her to the front of the bar, where she got her a strong coffee and called a cab. She'd drive her home herself, but knew she lived over an hour away.

"It'll be all right. Pain never leaves, but you can learn to live with it," Brett said when she helped Rosa into the cab a little later.

Chapter Nine

Now Brett had almost all the pieces of the puzzle. Jack was Chuck's uncle and set Chuck up in business so that Chuck could launder money for him. Also, Brett knew Jack's son had died back in Vietnam, so he didn't have a son to take over his business when he retired, which he'd have to do sooner or later. After all, none of them were getting any younger.

Brett also knew Jack had a daughter, Tina, but he would never even think of putting a woman in charge of things. It wasn't his style. He had had a problem with Brett's being in the business from the first time he'd heard of her.

So maybe he was thinking of having Chuck be his successor, which meant Chuck must've gone way overboard on his additional siphoning, and then lied about it as well. It would not be a matter to be taken lightly, but still, if Chuck was to succeed him, he would've had to add insult to injury to get himself killed.

What this meant was that there was a lot of money lying around somewhere. Even Chuck would've had the sense to do something else with it, at least until things calmed down. Jack would've noticed too easily if Chuck's lifestyle suddenly became extraordinary.

So Chuck turns on Jack and Jack needs not only to recoup his money, but also take care of Chuck and find himself a new successor.

She suddenly remembered Tony's mentioning that he didn't plan on being a hit man forever, that it was a young man's occupation. She loved it when the pieces fit together so nicely.

At the ski lodge that day she and Allie must've witnessed one of Tony's first arrangements with Jack. He was getting his first payment and orders, done under secrecy until they both knew they could trust each other.

So Jack had his new successor take care of the old one. Had Tony gotten cocky, Brett wondered, and that was how Chuck had gotten away, running for his life when he was gunned down in front of Allie and Brett at the Capitol?

The reason there were two men, Tony and whoever helped him, was that Chuck would've been suspicious if some stranger came to escort him to a meeting. Of course, it turned out to their advantage that there were two of them. That way, while Brett and Allie chased one, the other was able to grab the body and pick him up.

So she knew who did it and why, but could she prove it? Beyond that, the men who planted Chuck in his office were obviously looking for something, probably the money. Any paperwork at BB&B would probably only implicate Chuck, not Jack or his direct employees.

But that meant that until the money was found, Sara was in danger. Even though Allie had witnessed an amicable meeting between Sara and her husband's uncle, he was probably just biding his time, waiting to see what she knew, how much she knew. After all, he might be able to continue using BB&B for laundering, and why shoot yourself in the foot?

So what did Chuck do with the money? Rosa didn't appear to know. He could have given it to someone, Brett thought, hidden it somewhere — or, worse yet, did he do the old movie trick of mailing it to someone? Or maybe it had been in his office and had been found that night?

Then there was the chance that Chuck had something else on them. She had a hard time believing anyone could think they could just steal money from people who regularly carried guns, at least without having some sort of additional insurance.

She glanced at the clock on her desk:. 2:40. Which meant it was 2:30. She just got the clock yesterday as a gift from the Detroit newspapers, and it had already gained ten minutes. No wonder admen called these gifts "trinkets and trash." She was not happy to be back at work, but she knew it would be rather suspicious if she totally blew off work this afternoon.

Speaking of the heat, there they were again, apparently paying close attention to her whereabouts, especially after her two-hour lunch.

She strolled down to Sara's office, which was empty. Looking around, she entered and closed the door silently behind her. She ran her hands over the walls, then checked the bookcase, riffling through each book before replacing it in its spot. She checked the desk, tapping for any hidden compartments before opening the drawers and examining the contents of each.

As she was going over the furniture, removing each cushion and feeling it for hidden extras, she suddenly became aware of another presence in the room.

"You look like you've done this before," Ski said, closing the door behind her and sitting in front of the desk, facing Brett.

"So maybe I worked my way through school as a private dick," Brett replied, casually facing Ski as she pulled out a cigarette. Ski stood and lit a lighter. Brett pulled away. "I think you're mistaking me for a femme." She sat down on top of Sara's desk.

"I'm so sorry," Ski said, handing the lighter to Brett, who took it and lit her own cigarette, drawing on it deeply and blowing the smoke in Ski's face. Ski grabbed the lighter back and pocketed it. "I'm making no mistakes about who or what you are."

"Is that so? Then perhaps you wouldn't mind telling me."

Ski glanced around while the flush faded from her

face, as if looking for witnesses, for anybody who could potentially incriminate her before sitting in the chair at Brett's feet. "You're a criminal."

"Oh really, is that so? And just what has enabled you to make this fascinating leap?" Brett braced her foot on Ski's chair.

Ski was working way too hard to remain calm. "You're not who you say you are — both you and I know it. Now, the only reason you'd be lying is because you're covering something up. You've got something to hide."

"Maybe I'm just hiding the fact that I lied on my résumé." Brett stood and slowly circled Ski. "Or maybe I'm having an affair that I don't want my wife to know about." She leaned over and whispered into Ski's ear, "Or maybe I just don't want my brand-fucking-new employer to discover that once upon a time I was pulled over for drunk driving."

Ski stood face to face with Brett. "You're too pat, too cocky with us." She took Brett's cigarette and put it out, then leaned in on Brett. "Nobody acts like that with the cops, especially not if they know what's good for them."

"Or maybe," Brett said, pushing Ski back away from her, "I just always act that way with assholes. Now please excuse me, I have work to do."

"One last thing," Ski said to her retreating back. "What's your favorite Trivial Pursuit category?"

"Arts and literature." She turned to face Ski with a smirk. "There's a lot you don't know about me, detective."

* * * * *

"What an unexpected surprise," Sara said somewhat facetiously as she opened the door for Brett at five-thirty. They weren't supposed to meet for dinner until seven.

"You didn't really need to clean for me," Brett replied, glancing about the disheveled interior briefly before turning to look outside through the blinds. She had known since she left BB&B that she was being followed and was fairly certain Paul was one of them. After momentarily toying with the idea of losing her tail, she changed her mind and decided to wait. After all, she wasn't currently doing anything incriminating and it was possible they'd eventually come in useful. Regardless, she wanted them to at least convince themselves they were smarter than her.

"You'd think those assholes could have at least cleaned up after themselves," Sara replied, looking through the wreckage. Books were tossed carelessly across the floor, sofa cushions ripped open and their stuffing searched, knickknacks strewn from the shelves, furniture upended and lamps destroyed.

"Which assholes?" Brett asked, pulling herself away from the window to look at Sara and assess the damage herself.

"Jack's friends."

"Who?" Brett asked, remembering just in time that Sam Peterson wouldn't know who Jack O'Rourke was.

"Oh, nobody . . ."

"So nobody destroyed your home. Are you gonna call the cops?"

"No."

Brett waited for more as she pieced together a section of the sofa and had a seat. "Nobody trashes your home and you ain't gonna do a damned thing about it?"

"That's right," Sara replied, fixing shelves and replacing books on them.

"So was it also Jack's boys who killed Chuck?" Sara turned and fixed Brett with an assessing stare. "I'm no fool, Sara. I told you before that that was a professional job, as is this. Plus, your hesitation to call the police indicates that either you feel they will do nothing because they are either clueless or on the payroll, or that you are scared to do anything."

"You seem particularly knowledgeable about certain things. Is it a safe assumption that your prior employments had to do with less than legal activities?"

"What were they looking for, Sara?"

Sara shrugged and leaned back against the wall.

"If you think I've left a trail of bodies behind me, aren't you the least bit worried right now? And if I have a less than legitimate past, don't you think I'd be a little worried right now with the cops checking into my past and following me?"

"Which you are," Sara said, walking over to Brett and playing with her tie.

"Hmm, I wonder how desperate that makes me?"

"You tell me." Sara was now fondling Brett's lapels.

"Your husband was murdered, your house ransacked. Aren't you the least bit worried?"

Sara rested her head lightly on Brett's shoulder. "Yes, I am."

Brett lightly caressed Sara's silky hair. "What do you know?"

Sara sat down on the couch, her head in her hands. "Why should I trust you?"

"Who else can you trust? You know that for some reason, I need to find out who did this. You don't know the reasons, but you already know that I am obviously playing for keeps here."

"When Chuck and I got married, his uncle Jack helped set us up in business. Helped us put together BB&B. At the time, I just thought Jack was a really successful businessman. He lived in a nice house, drove expensive cars, drank good scotch — everything in his life was so good."

"But?"

"But a few years ago the police and FBI went after some people in Detroit, saying they were mafia. Both Jack and Chuck were very interested in it all, and I saw Jack's name in several newspaper articles about it all."

"Did you ever ask anyone about it?"

"No. I didn't want to believe it. But then I started thinking about how much money we always had, how much cash. Things were going so well with the agency and all . . ." She trailed off, resting her head on the back of the chair.

Brett sat on the arm of the chair, her hand on Sara's arm. "If only you knew then what you know now."

Sara laughed lightly at this. "Yes, that's for sure." She laid her hand casually on Brett's thigh.

"So what are they looking for?" At least she now knew that they hadn't found it.

"I don't know. The other day, after you mentioned its being a professional killing —" She paused and took a deep breath. "I thought about those newspaper articles and . . . and went to see Jack."

"What happened?"

She rested her head against Brett, who again began stroking her hair. "He said he was very sorry to hear about Chuck. He was his only nephew, and his son died years ago. But he went on to say that maybe he might have some business to send my way and that we might want to discuss it once I've had time to grieve."

"Was there anyone else there?"

"Jack, his wife Eleanor, his butler and some other man who showed up while I was there."

"Was his name Tony?"

"Yes, that was it. Pretty nice looking-man, with a really nasty scar on his cheek. While I was there I saw somebody outside watching us, and it was Tony who went after him."

"Him?"

"The guy that was watching us. Or maybe it was a woman? I just assumed it was a man, although I do seem to recall long blond hair." She looked up at Brett, their gazes locked.

"Where would Chuck have hidden something?"

"What do you mean?"

"He was hiding something. Jack's boys are looking for something. We need to find it."

"They've obviously already searched here and the office, but beyond that, I'm not sure."

"Did he have any really close friends? Anyone he would've trusted?"

Sara went to the bar. "You already know I've been having an affair. Chuck and I . . . We were the best of friends and I did love him, but . . ." She took a sip of her drink. "We each knew we weren't everything the other needed."

Brett said nothing.

"Our sex life wasn't what it used to be. We'd occasionally . . ." She again trailed off, obviously embarrassed by this admission. "We decided it was best to open our marriage to some extent."

"He had a lover as well."

"Yes. He did."

"Male or female?"

Sara laughed and poured Brett a drink. "Female. A younger woman. Much younger."

"Who was she?" Brett asked, taking the scotch. Sara's fingers brushed against hers a moment too long.

"Jack's daughter, Tina."

"Isn't that incest?"

Sara shook her head. "That's what I said, but he said it'd only be an issue if they ever wanted kids together, but they wouldn't. I think he liked having such a young, attractive woman after him, but as for her . . . She didn't love him. I always got the feeling there was something else she wanted from him." She was idly playing with Brett's suspenders.

"Tina O'Rourke," Brett said.

"Yes. Maybe he gave whatever it is they're looking for to her. Maybe he trusted her more than me," Sara said, a tear running down her cheek.

Brett took Sara's hand in her own. "Or maybe he just didn't want to involve you if he thought it was risky. Maybe he didn't want to put you in danger."

Sara looked up at her. "I just want all this to be over."

"I know. So do I." She ran a finger down Sara's cheek, wiping away the tears. "The person you saw watching you the other night at Jack's was my lover, Allie."

Sara sighed. "Why are the good ones always taken?"

"They're not. Rosa loves you, you know."

Chapter Ten

Thursday morning was Chuck's funeral. All of BB&B's employees were there, including Brett, who had brought Allie with her because otherwise it'd look all the more like she could be having an affair with Sara, or as if she didn't want her two lovers to meet or be aware of each other.

Jack O'Rourke was also there, staying near to Sara. Two women accompanied him. Brett thought the older one was his wife, the younger redhead his daughter Tina, whom Chuck had been having an affair with. She did cry profusely, resting her head often on her father's shoulder. They seemed like a very loving family.

Brett was almost surprised when Jack had shown up. After all, if he was using BB&B for money laundering, she'd think he wouldn't want the cops to know he had associations with the owners.

Of course, his presence had made things even more difficult on her. She had to try to avoid him the entire time, because he might recognize her. She thought she succeeded, but there was never any telling.

Much of the rest of the day was spent at the wake. Brett had always thought it a big joke that Catholics always got drunk after burying someone.

She noticed Ski and Paul at both the funeral and wake too. She was sure she had disappointed them the night before when she went directly from Sara's to her home in Alma. She and Allie had spent a quiet night discussing everything each had learned and what they were going to do with it.

"So you think Tina's got the money?" Allie had asked.

"That's about the only place left to look. Maybe I can try to talk with her tomorrow at the funeral, if she comes."

"That's the plan?"

"I think the plan needs a little more work. We can't just hand over what we have now to the cops. I mean, even if Chuck was laundering money, without any more than that, there'd be no reason for him to be eliminated."

"We need to provide motive and opportunity, at the very least," Allie said. "Right now we have proof against Chuck, but that doesn't do us any good."

"There's not a lot we got right now. But I think

we need to follow through on anything we can — like we got that flyer for the play tomorrow night." It was tomorrow's date that was circled on Chuck's calendar.

"So are you asking me out on a date?" Allie teased.

Brett pulled her into her arms with a grin. "No. I'm asking you to go, so Frankie and me can go visit Tina. I think we need to look at that last lead."

"Is there anything in particular I should be looking for?" Allie asked, kissing Brett's neck.

"Anything out of the ordinary. For all I know, though, all the plans have changed. Maybe something was supposed to happen there, but has been canceled. No telling."

The rest of the night was fairly X-rated, Brett remembered with a grin.

Now she was driving down to Detroit, down to the Paradise Theater. After she'd finished paying her respects to Sara, she had called Frankie, saying she was on her way. He knew where Tina O'Rourke lived and had insisted on joining her tonight.

She knew that tonight, returning to her old neighborhood, would be a challenge. She was both scared and excited by the prospect. She had felt like she was half dead over the past year and a half, not doing anything she should be, or wanted to be, except loving Allie. She had always had an image of who and what she was, and she hadn't been living up to it lately.

She pulled into the parking lot of the Paradise Theater and put on her cockiest attitude. Frankie's jet-black Aurora, which he had inherited from Brett

Higgins, was there. She nodded to the security guard, who gave her a strange look. She walked past the obnoxious blinking neon signs and opened the front door.

When she rounded the corner, opening yet another door, she heard the beeping that warned the clerk someone had entered. Just like old times. She walked up to the window just as Sal appeared on the other side of the thick bullet-proof glass, a bored look on his face. The bored look quickly mutated into a look of stunned surprise.

"Sal, let me in," Brett growled.

"Who are you?"

"You know who the fuck I am, asshole. Let Frankie know Brett is here to see him."

Just then a dancer came out of the auditorium. She glanced at Brett, then glanced again. "Heya, honey, long time no see."

Brett let her gaze drift over Expo's fine, slender, shapely stacked chocolate body. The only thing she wore was her smile. "Hey, babe, what's up?" Brett said, thinking of the times she'd spent with Expo. She was almost surprised that she didn't want her now. She belonged here, but she didn't. She couldn't imagine ever sleeping with another dancer.

"Nothin' much, 'ceptin' I thought you was dead."

"Now could I go and get myself killed without sayin' good-bye to you first?" Expo walked up to Brett, but Brett pulled away.

"Frankie said to come on up," Sal said as he released the turnstile and opened the door, a look of total confusion still on his face.

"Brett," Expo began as Brett pulled away and

went through the door. "Now that Kirsten's gone, I hope you'll have a bit more time for me."

Brett smiled at her and headed up to Frankie's office. It felt good to be home at last. Though suddenly she realized her heart wasn't in it.

"I knew you couldn't stay away," Frankie said as soon as she got up the stairs.

She looked at him, all six feet six inches of him, in his black suit, with white shirt and black tie. "Have you been watching *Pulp Fiction* again?"

"So what brings Brett back from the grave?"

"We've got a problem." Brett walked past him and into his office. She glanced around. It was much nicer than anything he'd ever allowed himself before in the way of an office.

"Yeah, I figgered as much."

She walked over to the bar and opened it up. There was a bottle of Glenfiddich. "Aw, Frankie, you remembered me." She turned and grinned at him for knowing what her drink was and making sure he kept it stocked.

"You and I both know you just couldn't stay away. This is your home."

She poured herself a drink. "Hell, who knows anymore?" She took a deep draw of the scotch. Leaning back against the bar she lit a cigarette. Frankie stood patiently waiting for her to continue. He was more than twice her weight, but he would always consider her his boss. The two of them and Rick DeSilva had built this business into what it was today. In fact, the business in its entirety was a lot smaller than when Brett Higgins retired, but Frankie owned it all by himself now.

"You know you don't hafta come with me tonight," Brett said.

"If you're in it, so'm I."

"You sure you know where Tina lives?"

"Somebody I've looked up to for quite a while once told me it pays to know too much."

Brett grinned at this.

A mile north of Tiger Stadium on Trumbull, just off the infamous Cass Corridor, the Trumbull Theater wasn't in the best of locations and, from the outside, it was rather foreboding. The actual theater was almost fifty feet back from the street and looked like it was probably once a carriage house.

The neighborhood was a fine example of Detroit housing in the area. Huge, three-story buildings, grand in their time, were falling into near disrepair. This one housed a collective of people, some of whom were students at nearby Wayne State University.

Allie was amazed, though, that there was actually new construction in the area, from new apartment buildings a few blocks north on Trumbull, to other commercial buildings on Cass and Warren.

She parked on the street and walked over to the theater. There were several women, both femme and butch, young and old, standing outside smoking, talking and laughing. She had briefly been awed at the number of cars in the street, but once inside she realized that the theater, which could probably seat about fifty, was just about packed.

She could barely hear the music, which seemed to have a refrain about "dyke-time," as she paid her admission and entered, looking around for Tony or somebody else she recognized, above the noise of both men and women mingling, sipping coffee and saying hello to old friends.

The stage rose above the audience by about two feet and there was no curtain. The audience sat on benches and a wide assortment of chairs in front of the stage. The theater was rather small, lacking the grandeur of more formal venues, but still had a coziness about it.

The lights dimmed and people took their seats. Allie hadn't seen anyone who seemed out of place, but decided to wait it out and enjoy the show.

Frankie parked down the street from Tina O'Rourke's house. It was in a nice enough area, Ferndale, which was filled with trees and older homes that were fairly close together. Although it was just north of Detroit, property values in the area had been dramatically increasing over the last several years because it was suddenly a hip place to live, as were other cities along Woodward.

Unfortunately for Frankie and Brett it was also the sort of place where two people casing a house would be noticed, as would loud screams or gunshots.

Frankie and Brett sat in the car for a few minutes, waiting to see if there was any activity at the house, which there wasn't. Then Frankie got out of the car and, skirting the house, neatly jumped the fences, once again impressing Brett with the grace of his tremendous body, while she jogged forward to the front.

She peered in a corner of the front window. Tina was sitting on the couch in a dark room with the light from the TV providing the only illumination. A large, yellow Labrador lay at her feet on the floor while she ate from a bag of microwave popcorn. Occasionally, as the lights from the TV flickered over her face, she would jump a bit in her seat. Brett guessed she was watching a horror flick.

Crouching low, beneath the windows, Brett made her way across the front of the house, occasionally glancing up and into the house. No one else was there. The side door was located just on the other side of the gate across the driveway. The unattached garage lay behind the house. Frankie was already at the side door. They nodded to each other, indicating that everything seemed good to go, then Brett eased the gate open enough to slide through.

Frankie eased open the screen door then reached a gloved hand forward to turn the doorknob. It turned, and he gently placed his shoulder against the inside door. This was too damned easy. Brett took the lead, slipping into the house. They were on a landing that led either up two steps to the kitchen, which had a closed door separating them from the rest of the house, or down a flight of stairs to the darkened basement.

The screaming from the TV stopped, as if it had hit a less horrifying spot that would work up to the next slashfest, and Tina spoke, apparently to the dog. "Okay, Dino, ya gotta go outside? Huh, honey?" Her footsteps came toward them as she turned on a light in the kitchen.

Frankie and Brett quickly looked at each other. Brett didn't like having to deal with a dog, although she had always gotten along well with animals. There was still no telling if Dino would figure out that they were threatening his owner.

Both Frankie and Brett drew their guns. Just like old times.

Tina opened the door and Brett stepped forward, brandishing her .357 with its six-inch barrel. Tina tried to slam the door, but Brett was too quick in blocking her. Brett shoved the door open, throwing Tina back onto the kitchen floor. Frankie neatly stepped forward and grabbed Dino's collar.

"It's okay, Dino, it's okay," he said in his best calming voice as he gently rubbed the dog's head and ears. Dino's tail began to wag. Obviously, these new people just wanted to play.

Brett stood over Tina, studying her. Her gun hung loosely in her hand. She slowly raised it to point directly at Tina's head. "Bang," she said.

"Wha . . . what do you want?" Tina asked, propping herself up on her elbows and slowly creeping away from Brett.

Brett crouched in front of her and reached out to run a finger down Tina's cheek. "I want something only you can give me." She wondered if Tina had yet recognized her from the funeral that morning.

Tina's eyes darted from Brett and up to Frankie. "If you had any idea who my father was, you'd get the hell out of here right now."

"I know who your father is and that merely makes this all the more enjoyable," Brett said, brandishing her gun in Tina's face. She stood and offered Tina a hand. "Now, let me get a look at you."

Tina reluctantly stood and, at Brett's urging, slowly turned around. She wore tight jeans, which outlined a nice ass and hips, and an oversized green sweatshirt with the sleeves rolled up to her elbows. Brett suddenly grabbed a handful of Tina's long red hair and yanked downward.

Tina fell to her knees with a cry. "What is it you want?"

Brett turned to Frankie, with Tina still kneeling before her. "I dunno, Frankie, whaddya think we should do?"

Dino was whining by now. "Lemme let this pupster out, then we'll see if she feels like bein' a good girl or a bad girl." He gave his trademark toothy grin and looked down at Tina. "Personally, I'm hopin' for a bad girl."

While he was letting Dino out, Tina looked up at Brett. Her eyes were clear green. "Frankie? As in Frankie Lorenzini?"

Brett caressed the side of Tina's face with her gun. "I don't see what difference it makes."

"You don't care who I am, who my father is, and you won't tell me what you want. We're just moving right along here, huh?"

Brett straddled a kitchen chair. "Tina, your boyfriend gave you something, and I want it."

"I don't have a boyfriend."

"Not now, 'cause your daddy took care of him. But before Daddy did that, he gave you something, didn't he, Tina?"

"I don't know what you're talking about."

Frankie, who had closed the door, locking the dog outside, walked up behind Tina and whispered in her ear, "I dunno 'bout you, but I don' like to see her angry."

"Tina," Brett began, "since you so obviously know

what your father does, then you shouldn't have a problem figurin' out what we're gonna do with you if you don't cooperate." Brett had done this before. In fact, she and Frankie had teamed up several times — working someone over for some purpose. She glanced up at Frankie and knew he was there, ready to follow her lead in their routine.

But she couldn't do it.

She put her gun back in its holster and pulled out a kitchen chair, helping Tina into it. She sat down across from her. "Tina, we've got some shit going on. Normally, Frankie and I'd beat the shit outta you and you'd tell us what we want to know. We're really good about workin' with each other and you obviously already know Frankie's rep."

Tina nodded, her face pale.

"Now, I've heard about you. Just a few words from here and there, but enough to think I know what you've been up to. Y'see, I know you've been fucking your cousin Chuck. And I don't think you really loved him like that, or else you woulda been more upset at today's funeral." Recognition passed over Tina's face. Brett hoped Jack hadn't also recognized her. "So that leaves me wonderin' what you were doin'."

"You think you know so much."

"Oh, but I do. I know Chuck was laundering money for his uncle Jack. I know he was gonna be Chuck's successor, because I know your father's opinion of women in the business. And if what I've heard was right, that woulda pissed you off."

"Who the hell are you anyway?"

"Oh, I'm sorry, please excuse my poor manners. The name's Higgins, Brett Higgins."

Tina's disbelief was clear. "She's dead."

"Then just call me fuckin' Lazarus, come back from the grave."

"Do ya think I'd let just anybody order me around?" Frankie asked, finding a soda in the refrigerator.

Tina stared at Brett. "You've heard of me, how sweet," Brett said. "Now, you see, I got this problem because the only people who know I'm alive are Frankie here and my lover Allie. I'm on the lam and the cops think I offed Chuck. Do you understand?"

"How?"

"Doesn't really matter now, does it? All you need to know is that if I tilt my head in just the right way, Frankie here'd trash your house. It really wouldn't be pleasant. Your nice TV would be smashed against the floor, your cute lil' Pooh Bear sugar and flour containers would be in pieces, your nice hardwood floors would be all gouged out. Beyond that, you'd be lucky if you could walk in the next week."

"Is this a threat?"

"No. A promise. Y'see, you gotta realize where I'm coming from. You're worried about hiding some money, whereas I know money ain't everything. I'm more concerned about keeping the cops off my ass. You consider what each of us stands to lose, and you'll realize I got a lot more at stake here."

Tina looked at her. "My father can't believe a woman can run things, though he does respect you. Did respect you."

"He and I got a history. He wanted me done one night a long time ago."

"I know a woman can do it. But he would never

give me the chance. He wanted Chuck to take over, but I knew Chuck couldn't. I figured that, through Chuck, I could run things, take over."

"What did Chuck have? What do you have?"

"Chuck tried taking Dad for a ride. He was laundering for him and started taking more than his cut. He was quite clever about it, but Dad finally figured it out. But Dad's no slouch, or else he would never have gotten where he was. So he found a replacement as his successor. Unfortunately for him, Chuck got a photo of Dad meeting with Tony."

"Tony Marzetti?"

Tina looked surprised. "You know him?"

"I know everybody. So Jack's worried about the cash and the pic."

"Yes."

"And you have both."

"Yes."

She led them to the basement where she had hidden close to two million dollars in several neat black briefcases, as well as the photos and negatives.

"What do we do with her now?" Frankie asked when they were back upstairs. "Get rid of her?"

"Nah. I'm reformed now, Frankie. I already told you that." Brett looked around. "But we can't just let her go, 'cause then she'll just go run and tell Daddy."

"We could tie her up real good . . ." Frankie began as he walked over to the VCR and pulled a tape from it.

"Nah," Brett said. "People have an annoying tendency of getting out of ropes, or calling for help or shit . . ."

Frankie popped the tape and looked at it. " '*Scream*?' " he said, then turned to Tina. "Is it any good?"

She nodded dumbly as he pocketed the tape and turned to Brett. "Brett, I think I got it."

It took almost no time to properly bind and gag Tina and get her into the car, then they whipped back onto Woodward and went up the street a couple of miles. He turned off onto Main Street in Royal Oak. Their destination was a neatly sided bungalow with a detached garage and fenced-in backyard. Frankie led the way up the lit path and, by the time they were at the door, it was open.

A fair-haired, lean man stood there. He was about six feet tall and wore a flannel shirt, jeans and leather slippers. Brett figured he'd be considered a real hunk by much of the gay male community. He slouched against the doorframe. "Heya, handsome."

"Kurt, I'd like you to meet a coupla friends of mine," Frankie replied. "This is Brett and Tina." Brett smiled and nodded as she led Tina into the house.

Kurt eyed Tina and closed the door behind the little group. "Oh, Frankie, are you getting into some serious kink?"

Frankie turned to him. "Kurt, I, uh, need you to do me a little favor. Ya see, me and Brett got some work to do an' we need you to watch Tina for a coupla hours." Brett noticed with amusement that he shyly looked down at the floor. He was embarrassed in front of his friend. She had never before seen Frankie with any of his guys. Usually he just fucked 'em and got rid of 'em.

Kurt turned and silently assessed Tina, bound and gagged, then Brett. "I know there's a story here," he said with his hands on his hips.

Frankie shrugged. "Just a prank."

Chapter Eleven

Allie hadn't laughed so hard in ages. Her sides just about hurt from laughing. She liked this play, this theater, this audience. She felt right at home here. She had almost, but not quite, forgotten to watch for anything strange to happen, but nothing had.

She was a bit tense during the first act, trying to watch for anybody she might know. But the play had slowly drawn her in, making her laugh and feel. The first act was a constant tease — always making her feel that the two women were going to get together, were going to kiss — back and forth, back and forth it went, the supposed seduction constantly interrupted by the flaming upstairs neighbor, the bitchy ex-girlfriend, who was kinda cute in her overalls with her attitude, and the male co-worker who was played by a woman in really bad drag. What the hell were they thinking about during that piece of casting? She could at least get the socks in her drawers realistically; as it was she looked like she had a constant hard-on.

But the romance part of it made her remember how it was when she and Brett first met, with the constant flirtation, the romance, the sexual tension, the wanting and needing.

At the end of the first act the two women finally kissed and Allie was so relieved she almost forgot to keep an eye open throughout intermission for anything untoward.

The second act threw Allie into hysterics. It went right over the edge and was flaming farce all the way. She did occasionally pause to fantasize about the leading ladies, but in her fantasies, they always slowly mutated into Brett, with her broad, powerful shoulders and deep eyes, eyes that had at first put her off until she learned to read and understand their shades and depths and the way they changed colors to match her mood.

At the end of the show, as the lights came up after curtain call, Allie stood and looked at her watch. Apparently her half of tonight's mission was wasted. At least she had enjoyed the show. The closing music, Sister Sledge's rendition of "We Are Family," almost drowned out any possible conversation.

As she made her way out of the theater and to her car, the cast was coming from backstage. She briefly congratulated the bad drag king, who was wiping make-up from her face. The rest of the cast quickly hopped into mingling with the crowd.

Allie was putting the key into the car door when she realized she wasn't alone.

"We were right," Tony Marzetti said, sticking a gun to her side. "You did come."

She willed herself to breathe, knowing that any fast movements might cause this man to panic. He was a trained killer, so she had no illusions as to whether or not he'd carry out his threat. She was terrified, her hands shaking, so she forced herself to think of her loving parents in order to bring herself the peace she needed in order to think. It didn't matter that her parents had been dead for years; they would always be with her where it mattered.

"Okay, Allie. It is Allie, isn't it?" Tony said. "You're driving, at least for now. Get in."

"You're pointing a gun at me, so I'm just doing whatever it is you want me to do."

Tony gave Allie directions as they drove. "Go over to Woodward and take it south."

Allie glanced over at him. "How'd you know I'd be at that play tonight?"

"Chuck knew about the play. We figured he knew a lot of things, because of what he said he had." When Allie didn't reply he continued, "He had pictures of Jack O'Rourke and me together. You do know Jack, don't you?"

"Not personally." Her palms were slick against the steering wheel. He was going to kill her. Why else would he be telling her all this information? She said a silent prayer and kept her eyes on the road.

"He knows you, though, so you should be impressed. He recognized you and your girlfriend at the funeral today. It didn't take much for us to go from there to realizing you two keep popping up — at the ski lodge, at Jack's house . . ." He trailed off, looking at her, his gun still in his hand. "When I first approached Jack about working for him, we had set up the idea of several little jobs, things so we could learn to trust each other. Tonight was one of them. But Chuck got photos of us together, that first meeting, and that threw everything off."

"Why are you doing this?" Allie asked.

"What? Grabbing you?" He fingered the long scar on his cheek. "I've come too far to be implicated by a couple of chicks. Even if one of them did work for Rick DeSilva. I ain't wasting any more time worrying about you. I know people, I know things. It's my job. I got lackadaisical with Chuck and it ain't gonna happen again. We, Jack and I, knew what Chuck might've known. There was too damned good of a chance that he would've known the original plans, that I was gonna get another assignment tonight. I wanted to follow through on it."

He was using Allie as bait. He wanted her, she realized, but he wanted both her and Brett. It was office politics; he wanted his new employer to see that he could handle things, take care of them on his own.

She and Brett were the only people who were really onto it all. He was no doubt playing a hunch when he came to the theater tonight, but Allie's presence told him he wasn't wrong.

She had no choice but to give him Brett's cell phone number. And she pulled over when he told her to.

* * * * *

Brett's phone rang. She and Frankie had been busy trying to convince Kurt that Frankie really was a computer analyst.

"Hello," Brett answered the phone.

"Brett Higgins, long time no see," Tony said.

She felt cold. "Tony."

"Ayup, it's me. And I've got somebody here who wants to talk with you."

Brett heard Allie's voice and stopped breathing. "Brett . . ." was all she got out.

"Where you at?" Tony was back on the line.

"What?" Brett answered, breathing again but unable to feel anything else. Tony had Allie.

"What city are you standing in?"

"Royal Oak."

"Good. You got fifteen minutes to get down to Palmer Park. You can make it."

Palmer Park was in Detroit, not far from the Paradise.

"What happens then?" Brett asked.

"You'll find out." With that, Tony hung up.

Brett knew Tony was hoping to catch her off guard, by herself, especially with the time constraint. She pointed at Kurt. "I need the keys to your car."

"What?'

"Don't fuck with me. Tony has my lover."

Frankie understood. He went to the kitchen and retrieved Kurt's keys. "She'll buy you a new one if she trashes yours."

Brett did some quick calculations. Tony was counting on the fact that in fifteen minutes she could not get help. She and Frankie raced down Woodward to make it on time. Before they hopped in their cars, Brett had given Frankie one bit of wisdom, "Follow my lead. If anything happens, I love you."

Kurt's green Beemer handled well, and for that she was grateful. Her mind was racing, trying to think of how she and Allie would make it through tonight alive. Her only hope was that she and Frankie knew each other as well as she thought they did.

Tony was pulling her in, planning on getting rid of the only two people who were likely to know he was the one that killed Chuck. He wanted to retire from his life as a hit man, to move into a more respectable position, and this was his chance. He was playing for all the marbles, but so was she.

She didn't know if he'd try making contact with her, or just do a drive-by shooting. She didn't know if he was alone or had help. She just knew she had to do what she could, which was to be there. Otherwise, he might disappear with Allie.

She turned off all emotions. She needed to be calm and rational right now.

She pulled into the lot, knowing Frankie wouldn't follow her, and knowing she couldn't look for him because that might give it away. She crouched low in her seat, hiding behind the BMW's tinted windows.

The Explorer pulled in a few moments later. Her and Allie's Explorer. It pulled in with the driver's side toward her. The window came down. Tony had Allie in his lap with a gun to her head. He gestured at Brett, indicating that she had to come over.

It was stupid, but she had no choice. He was using Allie as a block so she couldn't risk shooting. The only thing to do was go to him. She slowly climbed out of the car and took a few hesitant steps toward the Explorer.

"Nice to see you again, Brett," Tony said, then he opened fire. Brett dove for the ground and rolled. By the time she got up she could see Allie and Tony were fighting in the car.

She heard the squealing of tires as Frankie rushed in, but Tony had already floored it.

Frankie had already rolled down the passenger's window. She dove in as he drove past.

The bastard had Allie.

"Floor it," Brett ordered, rolling down her window.

"He's already doing at least eighty — if we take out a tire now, Allie's toast," Frankie growled, warning Brett that a vehicle moving that fast could easily lose control as it hit the I-75 on-ramp burning rubber.

Tony went even faster, obviously trying to lose them as he switched from one lane to another. Frankie kept on his tail, though, while Brett tried to line up a shot and develop a game plan.

"Floor it like you're trying to get up next to him, that way he'll stay in his own goddamned lane." Brett pulled up her gun, carefully eyeing the racing car in front of them. "I'm gonna take out Tony and then you pull as close to them as possible . . ."

"You can't fuckin' take out Tony — do you know what the fuck'll happen without a driver?"

"I'm going over!" Brett screamed.

She reached out the window and pulled the trigger, once, twice, three times. Glass shattered. The interior of the Explorer was awash with blood, like a body had blown up inside it. Frankie floored it but Tony's body must've lodged with his foot against the gas because she could barely catch it.

"Closer!" Brett yelled, hanging out of the window, trying to grab hold of the other car.

This was the best chance she'd get. The car was going out of control to the right. She threw herself out of the window before her fear could get the best of her. The wind hit her more forcefully than she had guessed. Tears stained her vision but her anger overruled everything.

She grabbed onto the steering wheel with both hands, her waist resting on the windowsill, fragments of glass that remained from her gunshots cutting up through the cloth of her jacket and shirt. As the car careened off to the side, she tried to change her grip on the steering wheel, but she felt her foot hit the hard pavement of the freeway they raced over.

As she tried to pull herself up she heard a crash behind her. Frankie had cut someone off to clear the path of the runaway vehicle. The dividing wall came racing up, so she brought her weight back up the sill, tried to correct the steering with her left hand and dropped her right hand to find a more stable point of purchase to haul herself into the car with —

She found the bloody mess that was once Tony's head and nearly gagged.

Suddenly, there was something there, something to hold onto, and she yanked onto it for all she was worth. Only later would she discover that Allie had managed to get her bound legs up to the seat, over the brains and gore that was once Tony, so that Brett could grab them and she could help drag her into the car.

Brett came through the window head first, kicked

Tony's foot off the gas as she tried to lean to the right to see out the window, which was coated with blood. She hit the brake and veered off to the right, once again narrowly missing the dividing wall.

The car came to a stop in the breakdown lane, and Brett looked over at Allie, not believing they were still both alive. She dropped her head into Allie's lap, laughing maniacally. Frankie pulled up and ran around to open Allie's door and removed her gag, then hugged her. Brett unsuccessfully tried to sit up, but still managed to briefly take Allie's face and kiss her.

"I love you," Brett said, never knowing anything more fully in her entire life.

Both Brett and Allie burst out laughing. Neither of them stopped for a moment as Frankie untied Allie's hands and feet and tried to massage some feeling back into them.

When the police showed up the two were practically lying across each other, and the remains of Tony Marzetti, covered in the evidence of his death, giggling quietly.

Chapter Twelve

"I can't believe you're hauling my ass off to see a play tonight," Brett said a month later as she knotted her tie and pulled on her jacket.

"Yes." Allie wrapped her arms around Brett's strong shoulders. "It's a fabulous play that I don't think any of you should miss. And it's got a really great ending where enemies turn into allies." *Just A Phase* had added an extra weekend because so many people had come to see it during its regular run.

"Uh huh," Brett said, holding Allie tight in her arms. "You're just lucky you're pulling this shit now."

Theater, opera, all that stuff wasn't exactly Brett's cup of tea.

"Hmm?"

"I was so scared I was gonna lose you."

Allie looked up. Brett knew her fear still showed. "It's all right now, hon," Allie said, wiping the tear away. "We seem to have found our way through to a happily-ever-after."

Sara, Tina, Rosa and Brett had been cleared of the murder of Chuck Bertram. Brett, Frankie and Kurt might've had a charge against them for kidnapping Tina, but Brett and Frankie's highly paid attorneys helped get them all out of the kettle on that.

Brett's lawyers were also trying to clear Brett of a manslaughter charge with regard to Tony. They were hoping to plea bargain either probation or community service in exchange for Brett's sharing information about Tony and Jack and all their operations.

Brett had quit her job at BB&B and discovered that, in all truth, the police didn't have any real evidence against her for her past endeavors. Any proof had been lost with the burning of the old Paradise Theater.

Rosa and Sara were moving in together. Sara had finally realized she broke up with Rosa because she was afraid of what people would say. She was holding the agency together, despite the audit the IRS had initiated.

Brett was willing to guess that Jack would get off, but at least he was temporarily incarcerated for money laundering and accessory to murder.

Tina was trying to take over her father's business while he was in the slammer. Of course, many key people were now missing, but Brett heard she was looking forward to rebuilding it with people she had hand-picked. Her mother tried to talk her into moving into her father's high-security home with her, but Tina thought it was a little too ostentatious.

And the man who had stood to lose the most in the trial and the situation, the man who was pegged as Jack O'Rourke's fall guy, had already lost it all. Tony Marzetti was six feet under, covered with a heckuva lot of dirt.

The upshot of all this was that Brett could have her name back, the name she had waited so long for, the identity she wanted, and she and Allie could move back home. They were currently staying in a hotel until they found a house they wanted to buy in the Detroit area.

Brett wrapped her arms around Allie, their lips and tongues meeting in a passionate yet tender dance. She couldn't believe how close she had come to losing this woman. She picked her up and carried her to bed.

"Brett, we're gonna be late," Allie half-heartedly complained, but Brett knew she wanted this as much as she did. She slowly undressed her, running her hands over soft, smooth skin, her lips and teeth finding already hard nipples, her fingers delving into warm, wet softness.

Allie opened up for her, and she went inside.

Later that night, during intermission, she, Kurt, Frankie, Allie and Madeline stood outside the theater. It didn't really matter what they were talking about, Brett just knew she was happy to have her own identity back, to be with Frankie, and to have Allie at her side. She was also truly happy Frankie had someone at his side as well.

And that was when she realized that as much as things change, they stay the same. She couldn't've been happier.

Epilogue

Brett knew where she was, even though Frankie had blindfolded her back at the hotel. If the walk, doors and sounds weren't enough to clue her in, then the smell of perfume and filth would have. He was taking her upstairs at the Paradise Theater.

He had her by the elbow and was guiding her, right up until he reached his big beefy paws around to take off her blindfold.

"Whaddya think?" he asked.

Brett looked around. The office was beautiful with a cream-colored textured paint on the walls, accented by two of her favorite Ansel Adams prints; the floor was real hardwood with a tasteful Oriental rug in its center. There were two large oak bookcases along one wall, and a large oak desk dominated the center of the room. The chair behind the desk was covered in real leather, as were the two visitors' chairs and the couch that ran along another wall. On the desk was a brand new computer. Brett figured she'd leave looking at that till later.

Brett walked up to the bookshelf, which was almost barren, and picked up one of the two photos on it. It was one of her and Allie at the prom. Brett had forgotten she had given Frankie some of the duplicates of the evening's pictures.

She was amazed at the years gone by, amazed by how young and in love they looked. Now they looked a touch older, but still in love.

She reached over and picked up the other photo. Someone had taken it of her, Frankie and Rick one night when they went out together. She figured it was taken by either Storm or Ted.

Frankie walked up beside her. "Figgered I'd start the decoratin' for ya, but decided to leave the rest of the shelves up to you. I know how much you like them books of yours."

Brett again looked around the office, this time somewhat wistfully. "I'd love to, Frankie, but . . ."

"I ain't takin' no buts, Brett."

She turned to face him. "Allie'd kill me!"

"I ain't sayin' ya gotta join me in business. All's I'm doin' is givin' you office space. I don' think you need to be workin' for somebody else. Ya need to be your own boss. You're good at it."

Brett ran her fingers over the computer's keyboard. "But what would I do?" Even as she said it, she could hear Madeline's voice in her head: "You will do what you are supposed to do."

A few of the publications of
THE NAIAD PRESS, INC.
P.O. Box 10543 Tallahassee, Florida 32302
Phone (850) 539-5965
Toll-Free Order Number: 1-800-533-1973
Web Site: WWW.NAIADPRESS.COM
Mail orders welcome. Please include 15% postage.
Write or call for our free catalog which also features an incredible selection of lesbian videos.

RIVER QUAY by Janet McClellan. 208 pp. 3rd Tru North mystery.	ISBN 1-56280-212-7	11.95
ENDLESS LOVE by Lisa Shapiro. 272 pp. To believe, once again, that love can be forever.	ISBN 1-56280-213-5	11.95
FALLEN FROM GRACE by Pat Welch. 256 pp. 6th Helen Black mystery.	ISBN 1-56280-209-7	11.95
THE NAKED EYE by Catherine Ennis. 208 pp. Her lover in the camera's eye . . .	ISBN 1-56280-210-0	11.95
OVER THE LINE by Tracey Richardson. 176 pp. 2nd Stevie Houston mystery.	ISBN 1-56280-202-X	11.95
JULIA'S SONG by Ann O'Leary. 208 pp. Strangely disturbing . . . strangely exciting.	ISBN 1-56280-197-X	11.95
LOVE IN THE BALANCE by Marianne K. Martin. 256 pp. Weighing the costs of love . . .	ISBN 1-56280-199-6	11.95
PIECE OF MY HEART by Julia Watts. 208 pp. All the stuff that dreams are made of—	ISBN 1-56280-206-2	11.95
MAKING UP FOR LOST TIME by Karin Kallmaker. 240 pp. Nobody does it better . . .	ISBN 1-56280-196-1	11.95
GOLD FEVER by Lyn Denison. 224 pp. By author of *Dream Lover.*	ISBN 1-56280-201-1	11.95
WHEN THE DEAD SPEAK by Therese Szymanski. 224 pp. 2nd Brett Higgins mystery.	ISBN 1-56280-198-8	11.95
FOURTH DOWN by Kate Calloway. 240 pp. 4th Cassidy James mystery.	ISBN 1-56280-205-4	11.95
A MOMENT'S INDISCRETION by Peggy J. Herring. 176 pp. There's a fine line between love and lust . . .	ISBN 1-56280-194-5	11.95
CITY LIGHTS/COUNTRY CANDLES by Penny Hayes. 208 pp. About the women she has known . . .	ISBN 1-56280-195-3	11.95
POSSESSIONS by Kaye Davis. 240 pp. 2nd Maris Middleton mystery.	ISBN 1-56280-192-9	11.95
A QUESTION OF LOVE by Saxon Bennett. 208 pp. Every woman is granted one great love.	ISBN 1-56280-205-4	11.95
RHYTHM TIDE by Frankie J. Jones. 160 pp. . . . to desire passionately and be passionately desired.	ISBN 1-56280-189-9	11.95
PENN VALLEY PHOENIX by Janet McClellan. 208 pp. 2nd Tru North Mystery.	ISBN 1-56280-200-3	11.95
BY RESERVATION ONLY by Jackie Calhoun. 240 pp. A chance for true happiness.	ISBN 1-56280-191-0	11.95
OLD BLACK MAGIC by Jaye Maiman. 272 pp. 9th Robin Miller mystery.	ISBN 1-56280-175-9	11.95
LEGACY OF LOVE by Marianne K. Martin. 240 pp. Women will do anything for her . . .	ISBN 1-56280-184-8	11.95

LETTING GO by Ann O'Leary. 160 pp. Laura, at 39, in love with 23-year-old Kate. ISBN 1-56280-183-X 11.95

LADY BE GOOD edited by Barbara Grier and Christine Cassidy. 288 pp. Erotic stories by Naiad Press authors. ISBN 1-56280-180-5 14.95

CHAIN LETTER by Claire McNab. 288 pp. 9th Carol Ashton mystery. ISBN 1-56280-181-3 11.95

NIGHT VISION by Laura Adams. 256 pp. Erotic fantasy romance by "famous" author. ISBN 1-56280-182-1 11.95

SEA TO SHINING SEA by Lisa Shapiro. 256 pp. Unable to resist the raging passion . . . ISBN 1-56280-177-5 11.95

THIRD DEGREE by Kate Calloway. 224 pp. 3rd Cassidy James mystery. ISBN 1-56280-185-6 11.95

WHEN THE DANCING STOPS by Therese Szymanski. 272 pp. 1st Brett Higgins mystery. ISBN 1-56280-186-4 11.95

PHASES OF THE MOON by Julia Watts. 192 pp. . . . . hungry for everything life has to offer. ISBN 1-56280-176-7 11.95

BABY IT'S COLD by Jaye Maiman. 256 pp. 5th Robin Miller mystery. ISBN 1-56280-156-2 10.95

CLASS REUNION by Linda Hill. 176 pp. The girl from her past . . . ISBN 1-56280-178-3 11.95

DREAM LOVER by Lyn Denison. 224 pp. A soft, sensuous, romantic fantasy. ISBN 1-56280-173-1 11.95

FORTY LOVE by Diana Simmonds. 288 pp. Joyous, heart-warming romance. ISBN 1-56280-171-6 11.95

IN THE MOOD by Robbi Sommers. 160 pp. The queen of erotic tension! ISBN 1-56280-172-4 11.95

SWIMMING CAT COVE by Lauren Douglas. 192 pp. 2nd Allison O'Neil Mystery. ISBN 1-56280-168-6 11.95

THE LOVING LESBIAN by Claire McNab and Sharon Gedan. 240 pp. Explore the experiences that make lesbian love unique. ISBN 1-56280-169-4 14.95

COURTED by Celia Cohen. 160 pp. Sparkling romantic encounter. ISBN 1-56280-166-X 11.95

SEASONS OF THE HEART by Jackie Calhoun. 240 pp. Romance through the years. ISBN 1-56280-167-8 11.95

K. C. BOMBER by Janet McClellan. 208 pp. 1st Tru North mystery. ISBN 1-56280-157-0 11.95

LAST RITES by Tracey Richardson. 192 pp. 1st Stevie Houston mystery. ISBN 1-56280-164-3 11.95

EMBRACE IN MOTION by Karin Kallmaker. 256 pp. A whirlwind love affair. ISBN 1-56280-165-1 11.95

HOT CHECK by Peggy J. Herring. 192 pp. Will workaholic Alice fall for guitarist Ricky? ISBN 1-56280-163-5 11.95

OLD TIES by Saxon Bennett. 176 pp. Can Cleo surrender to a passionate new love? ISBN 1-56280-159-7 11.95

LOVE ON THE LINE by Laura DeHart Young. 176 pp. Will Stef win Kay's heart? ISBN 1-56280-162-7 11.95

DEVIL'S LEG CROSSING by Kaye Davis. 192 pp. 1st Maris Middleton mystery. ISBN 1-56280-158-9 11.95

COSTA BRAVA by Marta Balletbo Coll. 144 pp. Read the book, see the movie! ISBN 1-56280-153-8 11.95

MEETING MAGDALENE & OTHER STORIES by Marilyn Freeman. 144 pp. Read the book, see the movie! ISBN 1-56280-170-8 11.95

SECOND FIDDLE by Kate 208 pp. 2nd P.I. Cassidy James mystery. ISBN 1-56280-169-6 11.95

LAUREL by Isabel Miller. 128 pp. By the author of the beloved *Patience and Sarah.* ISBN 1-56280-146-5 10.95

LOVE OR MONEY by Jackie Calhoun. 240 pp. The romance of real life. ISBN 1-56280-147-3 10.95

SMOKE AND MIRRORS by Pat Welch. 224 pp. 5th Helen Black Mystery. ISBN 1-56280-143-0 10.95

DANCING IN THE DARK edited by Barbara Grier & Christine Cassidy. 272 pp. Erotic love stories by Naiad Press authors. ISBN 1-56280-144-9 14.95

TIME AND TIME AGAIN by Catherine Ennis. 176 pp. Passionate love affair. ISBN 1-56280-145-7 10.95

PAXTON COURT by Diane Salvatore. 256 pp. Erotic and wickedly funny contemporary tale about the business of learning to live together. ISBN 1-56280-114-7 10.95

INNER CIRCLE by Claire McNab. 208 pp. 8th Carol Ashton Mystery. ISBN 1-56280-135-X 11.95

LESBIAN SEX: AN ORAL HISTORY by Susan Johnson. 240 pp. Need we say more? ISBN 1-56280-142-2 14.95

WILD THINGS by Karin Kallmaker. 240 pp. By the undisputed mistress of lesbian romance. ISBN 1-56280-139-2 11.95

THE GIRL NEXT DOOR by Mindy Kaplan. 208 pp. Just what you d expect. ISBN 1-56280-140-6 11.95

NOW AND THEN by Penny Hayes. 240 pp. Romance on the westward journey. ISBN 1-56280-121-X 11.95

HEART ON FIRE by Diana Simmonds. 176 pp. The romantic and erotic rival of *Curious Wine.* ISBN 1-56280-152-X 11.95

DEATH AT LAVENDER BAY by Lauren Wright Douglas. 208 pp. 1st Allison O'Neil Mystery.	ISBN 1-56280-085-X	11.95
YES I SAID YES I WILL by Judith McDaniel. 272 pp. Hot romance by famous author.	ISBN 1-56280-138-4	11.95
FORBIDDEN FIRES by Margaret C. Anderson. Edited by Mathilda Hills. 176 pp. Famous author's "unpublished" Lesbian romance.	ISBN 1-56280-123-6	21.95
SIDE TRACKS by Teresa Stores. 160 pp. Gender-bending Lesbians on the road.	ISBN 1-56280-122-8	10.95
WILDWOOD FLOWERS by Julia Watts. 208 pp. Hilarious and heart-warming tale of true love.	ISBN 1-56280-127-9	10.95
NEVER SAY NEVER by Linda Hill. 224 pp. Rule #1: Never get involved with . . .	ISBN 1-56280-126-0	11.95
THE WISH LIST by Saxon Bennett. 192 pp. Romance through the years.	ISBN 1-56280-125-2	10.95
OUT OF THE NIGHT by Kris Bruyer. 192 pp. Spine-tingling thriller.	ISBN 1-56280-120-1	10.95
LOVE'S HARVEST by Peggy J. Herring. 176 pp. by the author of *Once More With Feeling.*	ISBN 1-56280-117-1	10.95
THE COLOR OF WINTER by Lisa Shapiro. 208 pp. Romantic love beyond your wildest dreams.	ISBN 1-56280-116-3	10.95
FAMILY SECRETS by Laura DeHart Young. 208 pp. Enthralling romance and suspense.	ISBN 1-56280-119-8	10.95
INLAND PASSAGE by Jane Rule. 288 pp. Tales exploring conventional & unconventional relationships.	ISBN 0-930044-56-8	10.95
DOUBLE BLUFF by Claire McNab. 208 pp. 7th Carol Ashton Mystery.	ISBN 1-56280-096-5	10.95
BAR GIRLS by Lauran Hoffman. 176 pp. See the movie, read the book!	ISBN 1-56280-115-5	10.95
THE FIRST TIME EVER edited by Barbara Grier & Christine Cassidy. 272 pp. Love stories by Naiad Press authors.	ISBN 1-56280-086-8	14.95
MISS PETTIBONE AND MISS McGRAW by Brenda Weathers. 208 pp. A charming ghostly love story.	ISBN 1-56280-151-1	10.95
CHANGES by Jackie Calhoun. 208 pp. Involved romance and relationships.	ISBN 1-56280-083-3	10.95
FAIR PLAY by Rose Beecham. 256 pp. An Amanda Valentine Mystery.	ISBN 1-56280-081-7	10.95
PAYBACK by Celia Cohen. 176 pp. A gripping thriller of romance, revenge and betrayal.	ISBN 1-56280-084-1	10.95
THE BEACH AFFAIR by Barbara Johnson. 224 pp. Sizzling summer romance/mystery/intrigue.	ISBN 1-56280-090-6	10.95

GETTING THERE by Robbi Sommers. 192 pp. Nobody does it like Robbi!	ISBN 1-56280-099-X	10.95
FINAL CUT by Lisa Haddock. 208 pp. 2nd Carmen Ramirez Mystery.	ISBN 1-56280-088-4	10.95
FLASHPOINT by Katherine V. Forrest. 256 pp. A Lesbian blockbuster!	ISBN 1-56280-079-5	10.95
CLAIRE OF THE MOON by Nicole Conn. Audio Book — Read by Marianne Hyatt.	ISBN 1-56280-113-9	16.95
FOR LOVE AND FOR LIFE: INTIMATE PORTRAITS OF LESBIAN COUPLES by Susan Johnson. 224 pp.	ISBN 1-56280-091-4	14.95
DEVOTION by Mindy Kaplan. 192 pp. See the movie — read the book!	ISBN 1-56280-093-0	10.95
SOMEONE TO WATCH by Jaye Maiman. 272 pp. 4th Robin Miller Mystery.	ISBN 1-56280-095-7	10.95
GREENER THAN GRASS by Jennifer Fulton. 208 pp. A young woman — a stranger in her bed.	ISBN 1-56280-092-2	10.95
TRAVELS WITH DIANA HUNTER by Regine Sands. Erotic lesbian romp. Audio Book (2 cassettes)	ISBN 1-56280-107-4	16.95
CABIN FEVER by Carol Schmidt. 256 pp. Sizzling suspense and passion.	ISBN 1-56280-089-1	10.95
THERE WILL BE NO GOODBYES by Laura DeHart Young. 192 pp. Romantic love, strength, and friendship.	ISBN 1-56280-103-1	10.95
FAULTLINE by Sheila Ortiz Taylor. 144 pp. Joyous comic lesbian novel.	ISBN 1-56280-108-2	9.95
OPEN HOUSE by Pat Welch. 176 pp. 4th Helen Black Mystery.	ISBN 1-56280-102-3	10.95
ONCE MORE WITH FEELING by Peggy J. Herring. 240 pp. Lighthearted, loving romantic adventure.	ISBN 1-56280-089-2	11.95
FOREVER by Evelyn Kennedy. 224 pp. Passionate romance — love overcoming all obstacles.	ISBN 1-56280-094-9	10.95
WHISPERS by Kris Bruyer. 176 pp. Romantic ghost story.	ISBN 1-56280-082-5	10.95
NIGHT SONGS by Penny Mickelbury. 224 pp. 2nd Gianna Maglione Mystery.	ISBN 1-56280-097-3	10.95
GETTING TO THE POINT by Teresa Stores. 256 pp. Classic southern Lesbian novel.	ISBN 1-56280-100-7	10.95
PAINTED MOON by Karin Kallmaker. 224 pp. Delicious Kallmaker romance.	ISBN 1-56280-075-2	11.95
THE MYSTERIOUS NAIAD edited by Katherine V. Forrest & Barbara Grier. 320 pp. Love stories by Naiad Press authors.	ISBN 1-56280-074-4	14.95

DAUGHTERS OF A CORAL DAWN by Katherine V. Forrest. 240 pp. Tenth Anniversay Edition.	ISBN 1-56280-104-X	11.95
BODY GUARD by Claire McNab. 208 pp. 6th Carol Ashton Mystery.	ISBN 1-56280-073-6	11.95
CACTUS LOVE by Lee Lynch. 192 pp. Stories by the beloved storyteller.	ISBN 1-56280-071-X	9.95
SECOND GUESS by Rose Beecham. 216 pp. An Amanda Valentine Mystery.	ISBN 1-56280-069-8	9.95
A RAGE OF MAIDENS by Lauren Wright Douglas. 240 pp. 6th Caitlin Reece Mystery.	ISBN 1-56280-068-X	10.95
TRIPLE EXPOSURE by Jackie Calhoun. 224 pp. Romantic drama involving many characters.	ISBN 1-56280-067-1	10.95
PERSONAL ADS by Robbi Sommers. 176 pp. Sizzling short stories.	ISBN 1-56280-059-0	11.95
CROSSWORDS by Penny Sumner. 256 pp. 2nd Victoria Cross Mystery.	ISBN 1-56280-064-7	9.95
SWEET CHERRY WINE by Carol Schmidt. 224 pp. A novel of suspense.	ISBN 1-56280-063-9	9.95
CERTAIN SMILES by Dorothy Tell. 160 pp. Erotic short stories.	ISBN 1-56280-066-3	9.95
EDITED OUT by Lisa Haddock. 224 pp. 1st Carmen Ramirez Mystery.	ISBN 1-56280-077-9	9.95
SMOKEY O by Celia Cohen. 176 pp. Relationships on the playing field.	ISBN 1-56280-057-4	9.95
KATHLEEN O'DONALD by Penny Hayes. 256 pp. Rose and Kathleen find each other and employment in 1909 NYC.	ISBN 1-56280-070-1	9.95
STAYING HOME by Elisabeth Nonas. 256 pp. Molly and Alix want a baby . . . or do they?	ISBN 1-56280-076-0	10.95
TRUE LOVE by Jennifer Fulton. 240 pp. Six lesbians searching for love in all the "right" places.	ISBN 1-56280-035-3	11.95
KEEPING SECRETS by Penny Mickelbury. 208 pp. 1st Gianna Maglione Mystery.	ISBN 1-56280-052-3	9.95
THE ROMANTIC NAIAD edited by Katherine V. Forrest & Barbara Grier. 336 pp. Love stories by Naiad Press authors.	ISBN 1-56280-054-X	14.95
UNDER MY SKIN by Jaye Maiman. 336 pp. 3rd Robin Miller Mystery.	ISBN 1-56280-049-3.	11.95
CAR POOL by Karin Kallmaker. 272pp. Lesbians on wheels and then some!	ISBN 1-56280-048-5	11.95
NOT TELLING MOTHER: STORIES FROM A LIFE by Diane Salvatore. 176 pp. Her 3rd novel.	ISBN 1-56280-044-2	9.95

GOBLIN MARKET by Lauren Wright Douglas. 240pp. 5th Caitlin Reece Mystery. ISBN 1-56280-047-7 10.95

FRIENDS AND LOVERS by Jackie Calhoun. 224 pp. Midwestern Lesbian lives and loves. ISBN 1-56280-041-8 11.95

BEHIND CLOSED DOORS by Robbi Sommers. 192 pp. Hot, erotic short stories. ISBN 1-56280-039-6 11.95

CLAIRE OF THE MOON by Nicole Conn. 192 pp. See the movie — read the book! ISBN 1-56280-038-8 11.95

SILENT HEART by Claire McNab. 192 pp. Exotic Lesbian romance. ISBN 1-56280-036-1 11.95

THE SPY IN QUESTION by Amanda Kyle Williams. 256 pp. A Madison McGuire Mystery. ISBN 1-56280-037-X 9.95

SAVING GRACE by Jennifer Fulton. 240 pp. Adventure and romantic entanglement. ISBN 1-56280-051-5 11.95

CURIOUS WINE by Katherine V. Forrest. 176 pp. Tenth Anniversary Edition. The most popular contemporary Lesbian love story. ISBN 1-56280-053-1 11.95
Audio Book (2 cassettes) ISBN 1-56280-105-8 16.95

CHAUTAUQUA by Catherine Ennis. 192 pp. Exciting, romantic adventure. ISBN 1-56280-032-9 9.95

A PROPER BURIAL by Pat Welch. 192 pp. 3rd Helen Black Mystery. ISBN 1-56280-033-7 9.95

SILVERLAKE HEAT: A Novel of Suspense by Carol Schmidt. 240 pp. Rhonda is as hot as Laney's dreams. ISBN 1-56280-031-0 9.95

LOVE, ZENA BETH by Diane Salvatore. 224 pp. The most talked about lesbian novel of the nineties! ISBN 1-56280-030-2 10.95

A DOORYARD FULL OF FLOWERS by Isabel Miller. 160 pp. Stories incl. 2 sequels to *Patience and Sarah.* ISBN 1-56280-029-9 9.95

MURDER BY TRADITION by Katherine V. Forrest. 288 pp. 4th Kate Delafield Mystery. ISBN 1-56280-002-7 11.95

THE EROTIC NAIAD edited by Katherine V. Forrest & Barbara Grier. 224 pp. Love stories by Naiad Press authors. ISBN 1-56280-026-4 14.95

DEAD CERTAIN by Claire McNab. 224 pp. 5th Carol Ashton Mystery. ISBN 1-56280-027-2 9.95

CRAZY FOR LOVING by Jaye Maiman. 320 pp. 2nd Robin Miller Mystery. ISBN 1-56280-025-6 11.95

UNCERTAIN COMPANIONS by Robbi Sommers. 204 pp. Steamy, erotic novel. ISBN 1-56280-017-5 11.95

A TIGER'S HEART by Lauren W. Douglas. 240 pp. 4th Caitlin Reece Mystery. ISBN 1-56280-018-3 9.95

PAPERBACK ROMANCE by Karin Kallmaker. 256 pp. A delicious romance. ISBN 1-56280-019-1 10.95

THE LAVENDER HOUSE MURDER by Nikki Baker. 224 pp. 2nd Virginia Kelly Mystery. ISBN 1-56280-012-4 9.95

PASSION BAY by Jennifer Fulton. 224 pp. Passionate romance, virgin beaches, tropical skies. ISBN 1-56280-028-0 10.95

STICKS AND STONES by Jackie Calhoun. 208 pp. Contemporary lesbian lives and loves. ISBN 1-56280-020-5 9.95
Audio Book (2 cassettes) ISBN 1-56280-106-6 16.95

UNDER THE SOUTHERN CROSS by Claire McNab. 192 pp. Romantic nights Down Under. ISBN 1-56280-011-6 11.95

GRASSY FLATS by Penny Hayes. 256 pp. Lesbian romance in the '30s. ISBN 1-56280-010-8 9.95

THE END OF APRIL by Penny Sumner. 240 pp. 1st Victoria Cross Mystery. ISBN 1-56280-007-8 8.95

KISS AND TELL by Robbi Sommers. 192 pp. Scorching stories by the author of *Pleasures.* ISBN 1-56280-005-1 11.95

STILL WATERS by Pat Welch. 208 pp. 2nd Helen Black Mystery. ISBN 0-941483-97-5 9.95

TO LOVE AGAIN by Evelyn Kennedy. 208 pp. Wildly romantic love story. ISBN 0-941483-85-1 11.95

IN THE GAME by Nikki Baker. 192 pp. 1st Virginia Kelly Mystery. ISBN 1-56280-004-3 9.95

STRANDED by Camarin Grae. 320 pp. Entertaining, riveting adventure. ISBN 0-941483-99-1 9.95

THE DAUGHTERS OF ARTEMIS by Lauren Wright Douglas. 240 pp. 3rd Caitlin Reece Mystery. ISBN 0-941483-95-9 9.95

CLEARWATER by Catherine Ennis. 176 pp. Romantic secrets of a small Louisiana town. ISBN 0-941483-65-7 8.95

THE HALLELUJAH MURDERS by Dorothy Tell. 176 pp. 2nd Poppy Dillworth Mystery. ISBN 0-941483-88-6 8.95

SECOND CHANCE by Jackie Calhoun. 256 pp. Contemporary Lesbian lives and loves. ISBN 0-941483-93-2 9.95

BENEDICTION by Diane Salvatore. 272 pp. Striking, contemporary romantic novel. ISBN 0-941483-90-8 11.95

COP OUT by Claire McNab. 208 pp. 4th Carol Ashton Mystery. ISBN 0-941483-84-3 10.95

THE BEVERLY MALIBU by Katherine V. Forrest. 288 pp. 3rd Kate Delafield Mystery. ISBN 0-941483-48-7 11.95

THE PROVIDENCE FILE by Amanda Kyle Williams. 256 pp. A Madison McGuire Mystery. ISBN 0-941483-92-4 8.95

I LEFT MY HEART by Jaye Maiman. 320 pp. 1st Robin Miller Mystery. ISBN 0-941483-72-X 11.95

THE PRICE OF SALT by Patricia Highsmith (writing as Claire Morgan). 288 pp. Classic lesbian novel, first issued in 1952 . . . acknowledged by its author under her own, very famous, name. ISBN 1-56280-003-5 11.95

SIDE BY SIDE by Isabel Miller. 256 pp. From beloved author of *Patience and Sarah.* ISBN 0-941483-77-0 10.95

STAYING POWER: LONG TERM LESBIAN COUPLES by Susan E. Johnson. 352 pp. Joys of coupledom. ISBN 0-941-483-75-4 14.95

SLICK by Camarin Grae. 304 pp. Exotic, erotic adventure. ISBN 0-941483-74-6 9.95

NINTH LIFE by Lauren Wright Douglas. 256 pp. 2nd Caitlin Reece Mystery. ISBN 0-941483-50-9 9.95

PLAYERS by Robbi Sommers. 192 pp. Sizzling, erotic novel. ISBN 0-941483-73-8 9.95

MURDER AT RED ROOK RANCH by Dorothy Tell. 224 pp. 1st Poppy Dillworth Mystery. ISBN 0-941483-80-0 8.95

A ROOM FULL OF WOMEN by Elisabeth Nonas. 256 pp. Contemporary Lesbian lives. ISBN 0-941483-69-X 9.95

THEME FOR DIVERSE INSTRUMENTS by Jane Rule. 208 pp. Powerful romantic lesbian stories. ISBN 0-941483-63-0 8.95

CLUB 12 by Amanda Kyle Williams. 288 pp. Espionage thriller featuring a lesbian agent! ISBN 0-941483-64-9 9.95

DEATH DOWN UNDER by Claire McNab. 240 pp. 3rd Carol Ashton Mystery. ISBN 0-941483-39-8 10.95

MONTANA FEATHERS by Penny Hayes. 256 pp. Vivian and Elizabeth find love in frontier Montana. ISBN 0-941483-61-4 9.95

THERE'S SOMETHING I'VE BEEN MEANING TO TELL YOU Ed. by Loralee MacPike. 288 pp. Gay men and lesbians coming out to their children. ISBN 0-941483-44-4 9.95

LIFTING BELLY by Gertrude Stein. Ed. by Rebecca Mark. 104 pp. Erotic poetry. ISBN 0-941483-51-7 10.95

AFTER THE FIRE by Jane Rule. 256 pp. Warm, human novel by this incomparable author. ISBN 0-941483-45-2 8.95

These are just a few of the many Naiad Press titles — we are the oldest and largest lesbian/feminist publishing company in the world. We also offer an enormous selection of lesbian video products. Please request a complete catalog. We offer personal service; we encourage and welcome direct mail orders from individuals who have limited access to bookstores carrying our publications.